Lindsay's Surprise Crush

by Angela Darling

SIMON SPOTLIGHT
New York London Toronto Sydney New Delhi

If you purchased this book without a cover, you should be aware that this book is stolen property. It was reported as "unsold and destroyed" to the publisher, and neither the author nor the publisher has received any payment for this "stripped book."

This book is a work of fiction. Any references to historical events, real people, or real places are used fictitiously. Other names, characters, places, and events are products of the author's imagination, and any resemblance to actual events or places or persons, living or dead, is entirely coincidental.

SIMON SPOTLIGHT
An imprint of Simon & Schuster Children's Publishing Division
1230 Avenue of the Americas, New York, New York 10020

Text by Sarah Albee
Designed by Dan Potash

For information about special discounts for bulk purchases, please contact Simon & Schuster Special Sales at 1-866-506-1949 or business@simonandschuster.com.
Manufactured in the United States of America 0613 OFF
First Edition 10 9 8 7 6 5 4 3 2 1
ISBN 978-1-4424-8042-1 (pbk)
ISBN 978-1-4424-8045-2 (hc)
ISBN 978-1-4424-8046-9 (eBook)
Library of Congress Control Number 2012956187

"DID YOU HEAR WHAT HAPPENED TO NICK LOPEZ?"

A tingle rippled up and down Lindsay Potter's spine. She stared at her friend Rosie. "No! What? What happened to him?" she asked.

"You'll never believe it," said Rosie, lowering her voice to a whisper. Then she glanced at someone over Lindsay's shoulder. "Oh! Look! Sasha got her hair cut!"

Lindsay turned, trying not to show her frustration, and smiled and waved at Sasha, who was just stepping off her bus to join the throngs of kids milling around and socializing on the first day of school. She turned back to Rosie, trying to keep her voice even and not sound too anxious. "*What* happened to Nick?"

"Oh! Right. Nick. Well, I heard from Chloe, who heard from Jenn, that he—"

"Move along, girls, the bell's going to ring any

minute," said Mr. Drakely, the teacher on morning bus duty. He was herding middle schoolers in the direction of the main school entrance. Sure enough, the bell rang a moment later.

"See you fourth period!" called Rosie, hustling up the steps, her new purple backpack bouncing on her back.

Lindsay's thoughts were swirling as she made her way quickly to her locker. She knew just where it was—she'd had the same one last year, her first year of middle school. She spun the dial for her combination and wondered if anyone had managed to fix the sticky door over the summer. One yank told her no one had. Sigh. Another year with a sticking locker door.

Twang! The locker finally decided to open. She smooshed a few things into it and slammed it closed again, eager to get to homeroom to find out what had happened to Nick.

Nick was her best friend. They'd been babies together. Actually, their friendship was even older than that. Their moms had met in pregnant-lady-exercise class!

How could she not know what major catastrophe had happened to her best friend? True, they hadn't seen each other since June. She'd gone off to visit her cousins in

Cleveland for a week, and when she'd gotten back, he was already gone—first to baseball camp, then soccer camp, then some other kind of jock camp way out in the wilds of Maine, near where his dad lived. And when he finally returned, she had been gone again, first to music camp, and then her family drove her older brother up to college to help him move in.

Maybe Nick had broken his leg or something! She frowned. Maybe whatever had happened to him was the reason he hadn't returned her texts last night. She'd texted him twice, once to tell him they were in the same homeroom, and then again to ask him if he'd heard the rumor that Mr. Bates assigned homework to his homeroom students. And he hadn't responded. Was he in the hospital? In traction? No, he would have been able to text if he were in traction. Maybe both his hands were bandaged with second-degree burns or something? She swallowed uneasily. What a way to start seventh grade.

She walked into Mr. Bates's homeroom. The second bell had not yet rung, so kids were wandering around, chatting, hugging long-lost friends, and complimenting haircuts and new sneakers. She looked around the room quickly, trying to spot Nick. He wasn't there. Maybe something truly terrible *had* happened to him!

She saw Jenn, who waved her over toward the desks near the window. She also saw some really tall new guy who was surrounded by kids. He seemed to try to catch her eye, but she looked away quickly. She could feel the worry creeping over her.

"Did you see Nick?" a voice whispered from her right side.

She turned. It was Sasha.

"No!" she said. "Where is he?"

Sasha pointed quickly with her finger. A tiny giggle escaped her.

Lindsay followed her gaze. Her brow furrowed. What was Sasha talking about? She seemed to be pointing toward that new kid. He was a head taller than all the other kids in the room. He looked tall enough to be in high school. Was he standing in front of Nick? Lindsay craned her neck to get a better look. The new kid had really dark hair and broad, muscular shoulders. He looked really cute from behind. And then he turned around. He . . .

. . . *was* Nick.

MR. BATES CLAPPED HIS HANDS TWICE AND TOLD everyone to take a seat.

In a daze Lindsay allowed Sasha to propel her across the room toward a desk near the window, right next to Jenn.

How *could* that be Nick? Had he grown six inches over the summer? Or even *eight* inches? They'd been about the same height back in June, and it's not like she was *short*. Maybe he'd been an inch or two taller, but not much more. And now he had to be over six feet tall.

She flicked a glance at him and looked away again. He wasn't just tall. He had shoulders. And arm muscles. How could that possibly be?

Jenn elbowed her in the ribs. "Did you see Cassidy Sinclair come in? The girl who was new last year? She's going out with Nick, you know. Or anyway, that's the rumor."

Lindsay allowed herself to look up again. It seemed to be true. Cassidy was sitting next to Nick, leaning sideways, one elbow on his desk, her glossy, butterscotch-colored hair tumbling over her arm as she said something to Nick and then laughed coyly.

He grinned a little sideways grin, the same grin he'd always had. But now it was on a new face.

Lindsay resisted the impulse to rub her eyes with her hands and gape at him.

"Cassidy practically doesn't even talk to seventh graders," sniffed Sasha from Lindsay's other side. "Now that she's the megastar of the soccer team."

"She talks to Rosie," Jenn pointed out.

"Well, that's because Rosie's on the *soccer* team with her," said Sasha patiently, as though she were speaking to a small child. "She only talks to seventh-grade *soccer* players. Not mere mortals like us."

"Rosie told me Cassidy got drafted by some premier team this summer and now she's, like, a soccer goddess or something," said Jenn.

"A soccer goddess who is going out with Nick Lopez. Can you say 'stuck-up'?" said Sasha.

Lindsay nodded as if she were closely following what

her friends were saying, but in reality she was still trying to process that the kid across the room from her was Nick. *Her* Nick.

Mr. Bates was writing stuff on the board. Kids passed out study planners and random permission slips. Lindsay took hers from Jenn and passed them on to Sasha. She was still deep in thought. It must be true. He must be going out with Cassidy. Why hadn't he told her? They were practically siblings. They told each other everything. Granted, they hadn't talked or texted in several weeks, but that was because he hadn't been allowed his cell phone or Internet access in Maine, where he'd gone to his last camp.

A new thought occurred to her. Maybe now that they were in seventh grade, it wasn't okay for them to be friends anymore. Maybe he'd grown into a stuck-up person as well as a tall person over the summer. Is *that* why he hadn't answered her texts last night?

A low but audible collective groan rose up in the class, and she focused on what Mr. Bates was saying. He was explaining the All About Me assignment. All the seventh graders had heard about it—the eighth graders had done it the previous year, so most of the seventh graders were expecting it. There was her name on the board, slotted for a ten-minute oral presentation, complete with pictures, a week from Friday. She groaned too. She checked for Nick's name. There it was—scheduled for the Tuesday after her Friday.

She stole a glance at Nick, and found he was looking straight back at her. She felt her face flush. He pointed to the board and rolled his eyes at her. She felt her face get hotter. Her heart started thumping so loudly, she was afraid the whole class would hear it.

Stop it, she told herself. *You cannot act like a dork when your best friend so much as looks at you!*

After class, she hesitated for a minute outside the door of the classroom, checking her schedule to find the room number of her math class.

"Hey," said a deep voice above her head.

She looked up. It was Nick.

"Hey!" she said, smiling shyly.

"So what's up with—"

"Can you believe—"

They'd both spoken at the same time, their words tumbling over each other's. Then they both stopped and laughed.

Awkward pause. Lindsay couldn't help noticing that he smelled different. Like pine cones and maybe aftershave? Whatever it was, he smelled good.

"You first," said Nick with that sideways smile.

"Why didn't you return my texts last night?" she blurted out.

Nick looked confused. Was he pretending he didn't know what she was talking about? Or was he trying to think up a reason besides the truth—that he'd just blown her off? He started to say something when Cassidy appeared at his side.

"Nicky!" she said with a huge smile. "What field are you guys on this afternoon?"

Nicky? thought Lindsay. The last time she'd called him Nicky—about six years ago—he'd knocked her over and tried to put snow down her back. She had easily overpowered him, being taller than he was back then. She'd run away laughing but had never called him that again. Why did Cassidy Sinclair get to call him that?

"So what were you saying?" she asked, but Nick was smiling at Cassidy.

Oh, forget it, Lindsay thought. She pivoted around and headed off to her math class. Whatever. Maybe

Nick—*Nicky*—and Cassidy really were going out. Or maybe it was just a soccer thing. He and Cassidy certainly had that obsession in common.

Then she heard his voice booming down the hallway. "Hey, Linz . . . catch ya later!" She turned. He was saying it to *her*. Cassidy was practically glowering at her, with her hands on her hips. Lindsay waved quickly and kept going. Maybe they'd catch up at lunch.

Classes that morning went by in a blur. It was all about passing out textbooks, teachers talking about course expectations, deciding on seating plans. When she walked into English class fourth period, she was happy to see Rosie and grabbed a seat next to her.

"Did you hear Nick Lopez is going to be the starting keeper?" Rosie whispered to her while Ms. Haddam was passing out the syllabus.

"I thought that kid from last year, what's-his-name, is the goalkeeper," Lindsay whispered back.

"Kyle Grossman? Yeah, he was, but Nick beat Kyle out for the position," said Rosie. "It helps to be really tall when you play in goal, and Nick is now the tallest on the team. Plus he went to a goalkeeper camp and he's really good. You should see how far he can punt, too. At practice yesterday he was on fire. It's awesome. And everyone is talking about how hot Nick got over the summer. Is that weird for you? To see a kid you've been friends with your whole life suddenly become the Big Man On Campus?"

"Yeah, I guess," said Lindsay. "It's hard to think of him that way when I remember how he agreed to dress up like a princess with me when we were four."

Rosie giggled.

Just before lunch, Lindsay hurried into the bathroom and locked herself in a stall so she could pull a plastic tag off the back of her new blue jeans—it had been bugging her all morning. She was about to emerge when she heard a group of girls walk in.

". . . Nick Lopez is, like, totally amazing looking," said some girl whose voice Lindsay didn't recognize.

"I know, right? I heard the eighth-grade girls already voted him the hottest guy in the middle school, and he's only in seventh grade," said another.

"How does my hair look?" asked a third. "I think I need to defrizz before I walk past his table."

"I say we go sit at the table next to his," said a fourth.

In a fit of giggles, they left the bathroom.

What is going on with everybody? Lindsay wondered as she emerged from the stall and regarded herself in the mirror. *She* hadn't changed over the summer. Same old light-brown, medium-length hair. Still pretty but not superglam or anything. Unlike a lot of the other girls at school, she didn't obsess over the latest fashions and what labels were cool, and she didn't really bother with makeup except for a little lip gloss and, when she went out, a little mom-approved mascara. She was popular but not in the superpopular group.

Had everyone lost their minds? This was *Nick* they were talking about! The kid she'd played at the playground with since they were babies. The kid she'd played War and Spit and I Doubt It with, the kid she'd gone trick-or-treating with, the kid who weirdly didn't like ketchup, but who ate pretty much anything else you put in front of him. Then again . . . well, then again Nick did look pretty good. And she kept getting a funny feeling about him. What was going on?

As she walked into the noisy cafeteria, she decided to find Nick and make everything normal again. After all, just because the rest of the school had gone crazy didn't mean she had! He was still the same old Nick, and she had so much to tell him about her summer. She wanted to hear all about his baseball and his soccer camps, and whether or not he got to go to that Triple-A baseball game that he'd been so psyched about.

As she stood with her tray, scanning the sea of kids, she spotted him at a center table. He was surrounded by eighth graders, both boys and girls, most of them on the soccer team. There was an empty seat next to him, but after she started to head over, she stopped. Most likely he was saving it for Cassidy. Nick didn't seem to be looking for her. She suddenly felt self-conscious. Was Nick ignoring her? She didn't even try to catch his eye as she walked past with her tray. Luckily, several of her friends were looking for her. Sasha stood up and waved her arms from across the cafeteria, like she was landing a plane. Lindsay wended her way through the crowds of kids and plunked her tray down between Rosie and Sasha.

"Where were you?" said Sasha, batting her playfully on the arm. "We thought you'd never show, and we've been saving you this seat!"

"Ms. Trumbull is over there, making the seating charts," said Rosie, pointing. "We have to stay in the same lunch seats for the first week while she learns all our names."

Hearing that she had to stay in the same seat made Lindsay feel even more dejected. Now she wouldn't be able to sit with Nick even if he *wanted* to change tables or make room for her. She liked her other friends, of course, but she missed Nick. *This must be what childhood friends of pop stars feel like,* she thought glumly as she pushed her green beans around her tray. They must feel similarly lonely and abandoned when their friend becomes a celebrity overnight.

"There's Cassidy," said Sasha.

Lindsay looked up. Cassidy was carrying her tray over to Nick's table. Lindsay watched her shove her tray into the empty space next to Nick. Yep, he'd obviously saved the seat for her.

She stared at Cassidy, who seemed oblivious to everyone but Nick. She had a habit of tilting her chin up and shaking her hair back from her face, which on anyone else would have looked dumb and self-conscious, but which on Cassidy just looked, well, cool. Lindsay sighed.

She looked around the rest of the cafeteria. There

was Claudia, the Mexican exchange student who was in her homeroom. She was sitting at a table with a bunch of kids Lindsay didn't know, and Lindsay had the feeling Claudia didn't really know them either. She didn't seem to be participating in the conversation.

Things could be worse, Lindsay thought. She could be in a strange country where they spoke a different language.

After school, she waited by her locker for a few minutes after the last bell had rung, hoping Nick might pass by. Last year, they had often met up on days when they carpooled home. She knew he had soccer practice, but he might, just might, stop by, even for a second. He didn't.

She'd waited just long enough to miss her bus. "Thanks a lot, *Nicky*," she grumbled under her breath as she stepped outside and discovered it had begun to rain.

She sighed and called her mom. This was not a good start to the year.

THERE WASN'T MUCH HOMEWORK THAT NIGHT, it being the first day of school. Even after Linsday had done her math take-home quiz, memorized her Spanish dialogue, and practiced her piano for nearly a whole hour without being asked, she had plenty of time to socialize online with her friends.

The chat scene was a flurry of news about new kids, new teachers, and which boys had changed over the summer—with Nick, of course, being the star. Lindsay sat back in her desk chair and stared at the picture on her bulletin board. It was a photo of her and Nick as five-year-olds, all dressed up for trick-or-treating. Nick was dressed as a knight, Lindsay as a sparkly pink princess. Why did things suddenly have to be so awkward between them? Okay, so he had become cute. More than cute. He was totally gorgeous. She kept thinking about his smile, and the newly defined muscles of his shoulders, and his new deep voice, like warm honey.

"Stop it!" she said out loud. "Have you gone crazy too? This is Nick!" She vowed that tomorrow would be different. Tomorrow she'd go to homeroom and sit down next to him and talk to him like old times, and everything would be fine.

To prove to herself that all was normal, she texted him.

So are we going to work on our All About Me projects this weekend or what?

She waited. No answer. Her annoyance came flooding back. What was his problem? Why had he suddenly decided to stop answering her texts? Fine. *If he's going to be stuck-up*, she decided, *I won't talk to him either. Not unless he makes the first move.*

The next morning Lindsay got to homeroom early, but Nick didn't show up until just before the second bell rang. Mr. Bates made everyone sit in the same seats they'd been in the day before.

"I'll never learn all your names if you're not in the

same seats," he said. "In fact, would everyone please wear the same clothes every day for the next two weeks?"

Lindsay smiled. Maybe Mr. Bates wasn't going to be as bad as she'd thought. At least he had a sense of humor.

Mr. Bates asked Nadia Melek to read off the morning announcements, and then there was a sign-up sheet for anyone wanting to audition for the school musical. Lindsay hesitated for a moment and then passed the sheet right along. There was a small part of her that would love to try out. Sometimes she wished she were more sporty, or more willing to do stuff in public, like acting. It would be nice to have a hobby that everyone knew about and an automatic group to belong to at school. It was hard not being a jock and also not being in the theater crowd. There was nothing to make her really stand out. Barely anyone even knew she played piano, let alone that she was actually pretty good. She hadn't even played in front of Nick for over two years. It was a combination of being a little shy about it, and also worrying that kids would think it was dorky. Her older brother, Matthew, was *really* talented: He was an actor-singer and also amazing at piano. He was the one that people requested to play at family gatherings and stuff. Matthew was a superstar, and now so was her old best friend. And Lindsay was still just Lindsay.

When homeroom was over, she didn't even look in Nick's direction, and just trudged off toward math class, quickly wiping away an angry tear. What did she care if they were drifting apart? He didn't care . . . why should she?

She spent most of the day alternating between fuming at Nick and swallowing down a huge lump in her throat. By the time the final bell rang, her upset had turned to anger again. Fine. He'd changed. Whatever. She had to move on.

After her last class let out, she hustled through the crowds of kids in the hallway toward her locker to grab her Spanish and social studies books. As she worked her way against the current of rushing kids, she saw someone standing right in front of her locker.

It was Nick.

chapter 4

SUDDENLY LINDSAY WASN'T ANGRY ANYMORE. She was . . . well, what was she? Scared? Nervous? Lindsay's heart began thumping. Her palms felt wet and her mouth went dry. This was the kind of thing she had read about in books but had never felt before in real life. She felt like she was on a roller coaster. She calmed herself and took a deep breath.

"Hey," she said, trying to make her voice sound casual.

"Hey," he replied. "So how about that All About Me project, huh? Like we don't get enough homework—whoever heard of homeroom homework?"

"Yeah," she said, smiling and nodding a tiny bit.

Pause. She tried to think of something to say. But she couldn't think of a single thing.

"Did you have the chicken patty at lunch?" Nick asked.

"The what? Oh! No, I, um, didn't. I had the veggie burger. It was gross."

"Yeah. Looked pretty gross."

There was another awkward silence between them, even though the hallway was still full of sounds and activity—chattering kids, slamming lockers, and rolling backpacks.

She willed herself to come up with something, *anything* to say, feeling her face grow hot. "So, um, I have the same locker I had last year. The one that sticks. Want to see?" *Oh. That's brilliant conversation,* she told herself disgustedly. Well, now that she'd started down this scintillating path, she had to follow through and show him how the door still stuck. She almost forgot her combination in her awkward shyness, but finally she remembered and spun it around.

"Need help?" he asked, and without waiting for an answer he stepped up to her locker.

"That's okay, I'm used to it," she said, also reaching toward the locker handle.

Their hands brushed.

A bolt of electricity zoomed through her.

Nick's hand was on the handle first, and with a quick

movement he'd jerked it open easily. He smiled down at her.

"Thanks," she said, grabbing her two books and slamming the door again. "Guess all those new muscles of yours have made you stronger."

Horror filled her to her very core. Why had she just said that? She wondered if it was possible to die on the spot. She leaned against the closed bank of lockers, hoping a hole might somehow suddenly open up and swallow her.

Nick stared down at his large sneakers. The tips of his ears turned red. They'd always done that when he was embarrassed. And she was the one who had caused it this time! Awkward!

"Well, guess I should hustle," he mumbled. "I was supposed to be on the field, like, five minutes ago."

She had to rally. Had to make this okay. She called to him as he headed off down the now-much-less-crowded hallway. "Hey!" she said.

He half-turned.

"So do you want to work on these dumb projects together this weekend?"

"Maybe," he said. "But I have a big tournament on Saturday. And I think you're getting roped into the annual apple-picking fun." With a little grin, he loped away down the hall.

Lindsay started to smile back and then caught herself. Why had she *yelled* out to him in the hallway like that? Several kids' heads had turned to look at her curiously when she'd called to him. Clearly they knew who *he* was, but she was just a random seventh-grade girl, asking the studly jock Nick Lopez to hang out with her over the weekend.

She made her way to the school's front doorway. Today was her day to get a ride home. Every Tuesday her mom taught a weekly group piano lesson at the elementary school just across the parking lot.

"Hi, honey," said her mom as Lindsay dumped her heavy backpack into the backseat and then opened the front door and slunk into the car. "How was school?"

Lindsay slammed the door closed. "Oh, fabulous," she replied, rearranging the pile of piano books under her feet. "I don't want to talk about it."

Her mom was generally pretty good, as moms went, about not prying when it was clear that Lindsay didn't want to talk. She got the message now. "I forgot to tell you to ask Nick if he needs a ride home too," she said.

Lindsay looked at her. "He's on the soccer team, Mom. He's got practice."

Her mom shook her head. "Not today he doesn't. Marissa told me their coach had a teachers' meeting and that there was no practice today. Can you hop out and see if he's there? I figured you guys would be together."

Marissa was Nick's mom. Nick's mom and Lindsay's mom were best friends. Lindsay had known Mrs. Lopez—now Mrs. Diaz since she'd remarried—her whole life. Lindsay called her by her first name, and she called his stepfather, Alberto, by *his* first name. And Nick called Lindsay's parents Kate and Will. Nick had even taken piano lessons with Lindsay's mom when he was quite a bit younger, before sports took over his life. They still laughed together about how pathetic he'd been at piano.

The last person Lindsay wanted to go in search of was Nick, after having embarrassed both of them with her dumb comment about his muscles. And her mom's comments about them being together made her sad. But a part of her was dying to go find him, to have a reason to see him again. He didn't seem to know that practice had been canceled, so maybe she could catch him before he made it out to the field. With a small sigh, Lindsay opened the car door again and headed up the steps, back into school.

She knew where his locker was, of course, although the odds were against finding him there. But it was a place to start, anyway.

He wasn't at his locker. She set off in the direction of the gym, which led out onto the playing fields.

As she rounded the corner of the hallway that led toward the gym, she skidded to a stop and took a quick step back around the corner. Her heart thumped in her chest.

Nick and Cassidy were standing together at the other end of the long hallway.

She peered around slowly, careful not to make any noise or let them see her.

Yep, there they were. Nick had an arm propped up on the wall over Cassidy's head. Cassidy was leaning against the wall, talking and giggling and twirling a long strand of her hair around her finger. Had Nick lied about going to practice so he could ditch her to go meet up with Cassidy?

"What's up?" asked a voice behind her.

She jumped about a foot in the air.

It was David Costello. A sixth grader. A short, annoying sixth grader who had taken piano lessons from her mom a few years ago, before he took up the trombone and became totally obsessed with band.

"Nothing," she said shortly.

He peered around the corner to see what she had been looking at.

"Get back!" she hissed. Of all the people who had to catch her spying, David Costello had to be one of the worst. When he wasn't talking nonstop about how cool band was, he was asking a million and one questions. He always said the wrong thing at the wrong time, yet didn't seem to care that all the other kids found him so irritating. And he had the loudest voice Lindsay had ever heard come out of such a small body.

"You spying on Nick and Cassidy?" he asked her in a voice that was about ten decibels louder than it needed to be.

She pulled him back and put her finger to her lips to shush him. "No. Yes. Just a little. But if you tell, I'll clobber you with your trombone."

"Clarinet," he corrected her. "I do play the trombone, but the clarinet is my new favorite instrument." He grinned, displaying purple braces. A rubber band snapped and hit the wall inches from her head. "Oh, and by the way, I told Mr. Thompson that you were an awesome piano player and that he should make you play for the musical."

She stared at him in disbelief, forgetting, for the moment, all about Nick and Cassidy. "I am so not going to do that," she said. "I don't even play for my mom's student recitals. I don't play in public."

He smiled in a smug, condescending way. "You really need to get over your fear of playing in public," he told her. "You have to come out of your shell sometime, Lindsay. We're in middle school now."

She scowled at him, turned, and hurried back out of the building, down the steps, and into the car.

"*Must* you slam the door like that, sweetie?"

Lindsay didn't respond to that. "He's not coming," she said shortly, her eyes burning with indignation and embarrassment. She snapped on the radio, which was tuned to a Top 40 station, and turned it way up.

Her mom quietly reached out and turned it down a little. With a puzzled look, she started up the car and pulled away from the curb.

"Are you and Nick not getting along?" asked her mom after a few wordless minutes.

"He's a big, fat, stuck-up jerk," replied Lindsay.

Her mom didn't reply immediately, but Lindsay saw, in profile, her eyebrow go up.

Lindsay decided to go on. "He grew a little over the summer and now he thinks he's all that. Except he's the same Nick he always was. Actually, he's not. He's changed. He's a big, fat, stuck-up jerk."

Lindsay's mom sighed. "Honey," she said, "perhaps you shouldn't be quite so judgmental about other people. You've known him your whole life. People don't change that radically and that suddenly."

"*He* did."

"He might look different, but that doesn't mean he's not the same old Nick inside." When Lindsay didn't answer, she kept talking. "Or he may just be trying to adjust to what the rest of the world sees when it looks at him. It can be pretty freaky for a boy to look so drastically different so fast. For a girl, too, actually. So give him a chance, honey. Things aren't always what they seem."

Lindsay grunted.

They drove without speaking for a while, listening to

the song on the radio. A female vocalist was mourning the loss of her one true love.

"Part of growing up and maturing is giving people the benefit of the doubt," her mom added. "And you do have a quick temper."

"Says who!" Lindsay retorted. "Oh," she muttered, realizing she'd just proven her mother right. "Yeah, I guess I sort of do." She stared out the window. *Maybe having a quick temper is just part of my artistic temperament,* she thought ruefully.

They didn't speak the rest of the way home. Lindsay was grateful to her mom for not pumping her for more information. All Lindsay could think about was how Nick had lied to her. He'd told her he had practice. He *didn't* have practice. Why didn't he just say he was meeting Cassidy? There was no need to lie about it. Lindsay couldn't remember a time when Nick had ever lied to her before. It really hurt now to think that he had.

By the time they'd pulled into their driveway, Lindsay's mind was made up. She would stop talking to him. She wasn't going to be friends with someone who lied to her. Short temper or not, that was just inexcusable.

chapter 5

OVER THE NEXT FEW DAYS, LINDSAY FOUND MORE and more evidence to support her theory that Nick was indeed a big, fat, stuck-up jerk. On Wednesday, during lunch, Rosie reported that she'd heard that Nick and Cassidy spent all their time together, before and after practice, hanging out.

"I'm in his math class," said Chloe. "And he gets away with murder because Mr. Orben also happens to be the boys' soccer coach. Nick is, like, constantly late for class, or forgets his homework, and Mr. Orben just lets him goof off."

Lindsay almost couldn't believe it. Nick arriving late to class? That really did not sound like him. Then she reminded herself that this was the *new* Nick.

"My locker is two down from his," reported Jenn. "He and his jock friends do a *lot* of roughhousing and other annoying boy stuff, and Nick is at the center of the group. And he never gets yelled at by the hall monitors. It's like he's a celebrity."

And *all* of Lindsay's friends told her that rumors were swirling that Nick and Cassidy were going together to the fall harvest dance in two weeks.

"Whatever," said Lindsay, trying to act like she didn't care. "They're perfect for each other."

After their other friends had left to bring up their trays, Rosie looked at her curiously. "I don't think he's all that bad. You can't really blame him for becoming hot and a great athlete. It's not like he *tried* to do that. Besides, I thought you guys were, like, buddies," she said. "Aren't your moms BFFs?"

Lindsay shrugged. "I'm getting too old to play with the kids of my parents' friends. My whole life I've had to play with kids their friends bring over. I'm in middle school now, and it's time I chose my own friends."

Rosie narrowed her eyes at Lindsay, as though she didn't quite believe what Lindsay was saying. She always seemed to be able to read a different meaning behind Lindsay's words, even when Lindsay herself didn't know what the meaning was.

"Okaaaaay," said Rosie slowly. "To change the subject, let's talk about me."

Lindsay grinned. "What *about* you?"

"I have a crush. A big whopper of a crush. Have you noticed that new eighth-grade guy who plays defender on the soccer team? The tall one with the kind of shaggy long hair?"

Lindsay shook her head. "I barely know anyone on the soccer team."

"His name's Troy," said Rosie, sighing dreamily. "Troy. Isn't that an amaaaaazing name?"

"Sure," said Lindsay, grinning and rolling her eyes. But her mind was already wandering back to Nick. Was he really going to the fall harvest dance with Cassidy?

In art class on Thursday, Lindsay stood frowning over her painting, trying to figure out how to get her still life of a vase of flowers to look less like a little kid's finger painting. She sighed. She'd always been pretty good at drawing. But watercolors were something else entirely. They just didn't behave the way she wanted them to. The colors kept running into one another. Someone behind her said something under her breath. It was Cassidy.

"What did you say?" Lindsay asked.

"I said, 'That's awesome,'" said Cassidy innocently, quickly gesturing toward Lindsay's painting.

"Thanks," said Lindsay cautiously. She waited to see what Cassidy wanted. She and Cassidy shared both homeroom and art class, but this was the first time Cassidy had ever spoken to her.

"That's such a cute skirt. Where'd you get it?"

Lindsay narrowed her eyes suspiciously. Was Cassidy serious? "Actually it used to be my mom's. She wore it back in college and I kind of liked the color."

"Vintage. Awesome," said Cassidy. But her tone sounded kind of flat, like she didn't think it was awesome at all.

Lindsay tried not to notice that Cassidy had on the exact same outfit she had seen on the cover of this really cool clothes catalog—from her hair clip to her striped shirt to her red corduroys, all the way down to her black faux-leopard flats. Except Cassidy looked better than the model had looked.

"So yeah," said Cassidy. "Nicky told me the two of you used to be best friends when you were little."

Lindsay felt a flash of irritation, but she tried not to

show it. They *used* to be best friends. When they were little. Which means not now. "Yeah," she replied slowly.

"So maybe you know what his favorite color is?"

"Why? Are you knitting him a sweater?" asked Lindsay. She couldn't help herself. She knew she was being snarky, but she didn't care.

"Yeah, right, as if," said Cassidy with a tinkly laugh. She didn't seem to know that Lindsay was being sarcastic. "No, it's for the tournament on Saturday. We're all going on one big bus and so some of us were going to decorate each of the windows with different players' numbers and I wanted to do his in his favorite color."

"Oh. Well, back when we were little kids, when we used to be best friends, it used to be blue," said Lindsay bitterly.

"Awesome! Thanks!" said Cassidy, flashing her brilliant smile. She headed back to her own painting.

Lindsay dipped her brush into the dark brown and swashed it over half of her painting. She didn't even care.

On Friday Nick was standing at her locker when she came to grab her social studies book after lunch. She blinked at him in surprise.

"Hi," he said, his arms folded, his body blocking her locker.

"Hi," she replied cautiously.

"How come you've been acting so unfriendly all the time?"

Her eyes widened with surprise. "Me? *I'm* unfriendly?"

He waited, scowling down at her.

She suddenly lost her ability to think clearly. Her brain was all muddled. The hall was noisy and crowded, and she was aware of several kids passing by and looking at them curiously.

"I'm not unfriendly," she managed to stammer out weakly. "You're the one who doesn't answer texts."

He looked at her in confusion. Then he rolled his eyes. "Oh, yeah. You asked me about that the other day, too. Ellie took my phone and played games on it and the battery went dead. And then she lost the charger and we looked all over for it and then two days later my mom found it in Ellie's dollhouse."

Now it was Lindsay's turn to cross her arms and frown at him. "I don't even know why I should believe you," she said.

His face darkened. "What? Are you saying I'm *lying* about that?"

She shrugged. “Well, given your history . . .” She trailed off.

He looked at her, dumbfounded and hurt. Then he shook his head. “Whatever. I have to get to class,” he said, and strode away.

A lump rose in her throat. Why had she been so mean to him? This was Nick! She spun the dial on her locker, jerked open her stuck locker door, and grabbed her book, not sure if she was more furious at herself or at him. He deserved it, didn’t he? She hoped he and Cassidy would get rained on at their tournament tomorrow and her cute window that she decorated for him would become one big blob of blue.

Chapter 6

LINDSAY AWOKE GRADUALLY SATURDAY MORNING to the delicious smells of bacon and toast and coffee. She didn't like the taste of coffee, but there was something so heavenly about the smell of it brewing, especially when it was a Saturday morning and you could lounge in bed. But what was that loud pattering sound?

She turned toward the window to see rain streaming down the pane. She glanced at the clock. Almost ten. *Hah.* She sat up. Nick and Cassidy must be drenched right about now. She smiled at the thought.

The door opened slowly and she saw her mother peer in.

"It's okay, Mom, I'm awake," she said. "It smells good down there!"

Her mom came in and sat down on the bed. "Well, I have no lessons today," she said, "because two of my students are at the big soccer tournament, one is sick, and one is away for the weekend. With Matthew off at college now, I couldn't think what to do with myself with all my free time, so I made bacon! Better hurry down, though. Daddy is working his way through most of it."

"So I guess we're not going apple picking with the Lopez-Diazes, huh," said Lindsay, gesturing toward the rain outside.

"Oh, right, forgot to tell you," said her mom. "We moved it to tomorrow. The weather is supposed to be clear, and we wanted Nick to be able to join us. And Marissa and Alberto wanted to watch him play today, anyway, now that he's the starting goalkeeper."

Lindsay groaned. She was going to spend a whole day with Nick, after the kind-of, sort-of fight they'd had yesterday?

Her mom put a hand on her leg over the coverlet. "Are you guys still having a tough time?" she asked, looking worried.

"No, everything's fine with Nick," said Lindsay. It seemed to be a reflex she and all her friends had developed once they got to middle school—to tell their parents everything was fine, no matter how not fine things actually were. "It's just that I have a big project that's due next Friday, so I need to work on it this weekend."

"Well, today's a perfect rainy day to do it!" said her mother brightly. "And you can practice double time for your lesson, too!" She stood up and flicked the covers off Lindsay. "Rise and shine, darlin'!"

Lindsay spent the rest of the morning sorting through the pictures on her mom's computer, trying to decide which ones to include from her childhood for her All About Me project. Practically every decent shot was of her and Nick together. Every birthday, every vacation, everything she could possibly talk about during her presentation seemed to involve Nick. And no wonder. Marissa was practically her second mother. When Lindsay's parents had to go out of town when Lindsay's grandmother broke her hip a couple of years ago, Lindsay and her brother, Matthew, had stayed with the Lopez-Diazes for a whole week. They'd carpooled everywhere ever since she and Nick were in car seats together. How was she going to give this presentation without mentioning Nick a million times? Nick, who was barely even her friend anymore. Nick, who now appeared to be the most popular boy in the school. Nick, who may well be a big, fat, stuck-up jerk.

She felt sorry for herself for a minute. Then she thought about it. It wasn't like she was a total loser. She was pretty well-liked, she realized, when she thought about it objectively. But she wasn't in the popularity stratosphere like Cassidy Sinclair. And most kids at school didn't have any idea that Lindsay and Nick were so close. The two of them revolved in such different circles—he in the jock crowd, she in the smart-popular set. It wasn't like they walked around school holding hands, like they used to do in nursery school.

She was really nervous about her presentation. She hated public speaking. Public *anything*. And of course Cassidy would be sitting right there in homeroom, listening to her whole presentation and probably making fun of her for living in the past. And Nick. She cringed. What would Nick be thinking as she showed adorable baby pictures of him in front of everybody?

"Aw, look at this one!" said her mom, who had wandered in and was leaning over her shoulder, peering at the pictures on the screen. "That is soooo adorable."

It was a picture of her and Nick, aged about one and a half, in a bathtub together. They were both splashing the water by slapping the surface of it with their hands, and they were laughing their heads off. You couldn't see anything, but you knew they were naked.

"Mom. If I show that picture, I might as well join the witness protection program and disappear," she said. She couldn't explain to her mom how hard this project was turning out to be. She just wouldn't understand. It had been a million years since her mother had been in middle school.

"Marissa has been telling me the girls are calling and texting Nick nonstop," said her mother. "Think of that! Little Nicky!" She shook her head. "Hard to believe."

Lindsay felt the same stupid lump rise in her throat. It was like a golf ball had lodged there on a semipermanent basis. "Yeah, little Nicky," she echoed. "Well, I think I have enough pictures now," she said. "Thanks, Mom. Guess I should go practice."

Lindsay's mom got the hint. She really was an awesome mom, when you got right down to it. "Okay, honey," she said, kissing Lindsay on the top of her head.

Lindsay headed for the piano and sat down on the bench, staring at her scale book. How was she going to do this All About Me project and not seem like a pathetic Nick worshipper, like half the girls in the seventh grade? She so wasn't like those girls. She really *knew* him. She'd cared about him before he became the cutest, most popular boy at school.

Her fingers began moving slowly up the keyboard, playing the B-flat major scale. Two octaves up, two octaves back down, then ending with the chords and arpeggios. She knew the exercise so well, she didn't have to think about what her fingers were doing. Her social life, though—that was different. Why did it have to be so complicated?

Chapter 7

SUNDAY MORNING DAWNED BRIGHT AND SUNNY. Lindsay was awakened early by a bird *cheep-cheep-cheeping* on a branch right outside her window.

"Stupid bird," she grumbled, glaring at the clock, which read 7:17 a.m. "It's September. Weren't you supposed to fly south by this time?"

She rose, showered, and then faced the issue of what to wear for apple picking with Nick. Casual, of course. But how nice should she really look? How much did she care? He'd obviously seen her a million times when she was not looking her best. But that was before. Back when they were kids. Things were different now. She cared how she looked around him. She was confused again. Why did she care? Wasn't she still angry at him?

An hour later, after she'd tried on about seven different outfit combinations, her dad knocked on the door.

"Linz! Up and at 'em! What are you doing—crocheting yourself a new sweater? We're out the door in twenty minutes and you need to eat something!"

"Five minutes!" she called, her voice muffled from inside her closet, where she was on hands and knees searching for shoes.

Half an hour later, she appeared in the kitchen. Her father frowned and tapped his foot. "Here," he said. "I toasted you a bagel." He stared at her outfit. "Aren't you a little dressed up for apple picking, honey?"

Her mother strode over and put an arm around her. "She looks beautiful," she said quickly. "Now let's go."

Lindsay looked down at her outfit in a panic. Was she overdressed? She had on her new jeggings, her favorite red sweater, and her new boots. And she'd washed and blow-dried her hair. Her dad was right. She looked like she'd tried too hard. "I'm going to run upstairs and change," she announced.

"No, you're not," said her father, firmly propelling her toward the door. "We were supposed to be at their house ten minutes ago."

With a sigh, Lindsay allowed herself to be guided out to the car. How would he react when he saw her? Would he ignore her? Or would he pretend things were normal for the sake of their parents?

When they pulled into Nick's driveway five minutes later, everyone but Nick was outside. A cold fear clutched Lindsay's heart. Maybe he wasn't coming! She realized how disappointed she felt.

"Lindsay!" shrieked Nick's five-year-old half sister, Ellie, hurling herself into Lindsay's arms. "You look so pretty! And your hair smells all nice!"

"You certainly do look pretty, sweetie," said Marissa, giving Lindsay a hug. "I haven't seen you all summer, and look how beautiful you've become! You could be a model!"

Lindsay flushed. Then she noticed her dad staring toward the house, and she looked up. Nick was emerging.

"Holy cow!" said Lindsay's dad. "He's grown a foot!"

"Not quite," said Nick's stepdad, Alberto, grinning. "But probably at least seven inches. He's taller than I am now. And his feet are two sizes bigger than mine, so he's still growing!"

Now it was Nick's turn to scuff his foot awkwardly and go red around his ears. So far he hadn't even looked Lindsay's way. He had on jeans, a loose plaid flannel shirt, and a baseball cap turned backward. It was a breathtaking sight.

Lindsay had to look away quickly, as though she'd been staring at the sun. How had she never noticed how his dark-brown hair curled around his ears? Or how his coffee-brown eyes had flecks of gold and green in them? Actually, she had noticed that, about ten years ago, and had remarked on it constantly to him, telling him how weird it was. But now it wasn't weird. It was awesome.

There was an awkward silence. To Lindsay it felt like it lasted a week. Then, fortunately, Ellie grabbed her hand and dragged her toward the minivan. "Let's go! Let's go!" she said. "I get to sit next to pretty Lindsay!"

There was more awkwardness after Lindsay got into the way back and Alberto put Ellie's booster seat in so that Ellie could sit next to her. Ellie climbed in and Lindsay helped click her seat belt.

Was Nick too tall for the way back? Would he sit in the middle seat? But without waiting to be asked, Nick clambered into the way back with Ellie and Lindsay and clicked in. His long legs were comically folded up, like a carpenter's ruler, but he didn't seem to mind.

"Are you guys going to take me on the hayride yes

please?" asked Ellie, oblivious to the strained energy between Lindsay and Nick.

"Sure," said Lindsay with a smile. Out of the corner of her eye she could feel Nick steal a glance at her. Was he wondering why her hair was all done on a Sunday? Oh, she should have just put it in a ponytail. Awkward, awkward. She shouldn't have come. She should have feigned appendicitis.

Ellie began singing the songs she'd been learning in kindergarten, which eased some of the tension in the way back of the car. The grown-ups all chatted together farther up. Lindsay stared out of her window at the passing houses. They got to the end of Nick's street and turned down the road that headed out of town, toward the surrounding farms.

She tuned in to the grown-up conversation. The Lopez-Diazes were talking about the soccer tournament yesterday.

"Yes, we got soaked," said Marissa ruefully, "but Nick played so well, considering the wet weather."

"Rain is brutal for goalkeepers," chimed in Alberto. "But our boy has good hands."

Lindsay darted a glance at Nick's hands. He was

checking sports scores on his phone. He did have good hands, she was forced to agree.

"Nick's team won!" continued Marissa. "And I believe the girls' team came in second!"

"Tell them what else," Alberto prodded his wife.

"Nick got MVP," Marissa said proudly.

Lindsay could sense Nick squirming uncomfortably in his seat. He'd always hated being talked about.

"And another Central Falls middle schooler got MVP for the girls," added Marissa. "Cassidy. What's her last name, Berto?"

"Sinclair," Nick's stepfather replied. "She's a beautiful girl."

Lindsay suddenly froze, listening intently.

"And she can really play," added Alberto. Nick's stepdad was a huge fan of soccer. He'd even played semiprofessionally back when he was younger. "Strong and quick, and a real nose for the ball."

"We offered her a ride home," said Marissa, "since her parents weren't able to make the tournament. We took the kids to dinner because they were starving. She's very sweet. And you should see the hair on this girl! I'm embarrassed to admit it, but I was feeling envious of her long, gorgeous blond hair. Ah, youth."

Lindsay's mom laughed.

Lindsay sank deeper into her seat, feeling more and more miserable. So Nick and Cassidy had gone to dinner together last night. She wondered if they'd sat at a separate table, apart from the grown-ups. She and Nick and her brother had done that a few times when the two families had been out to dinner together.

Luckily Ellie chose that moment to insist that Lindsay and Nick join her in a round of "Row, Row, Row Your Boat," which eased the tension. It was doubly funny because Lindsay sang an octave below Ellie, and Nick sang *two* octaves lower.

Apple picking turned out to be fun. Nick even started acting like the old days, joking around with her, unexpectedly tossing apples for her to catch, lifting Ellie high over his head to pick the most perfect, ripe-looking fruit. Things felt almost normal.

"Hey, congratulations on your MVP yesterday," said Lindsay as they lugged their heavy bags of apples over to the small farm shop to be weighed. She was wishing she'd worn her comfortable sneakers rather than her fashionable boots.

"Thanks," he said. "I just had some lucky saves, is all. The guys on my team all played really great." He reached down and picked up Lindsay's bag to carry, as though it weighed nothing. Lindsay started to protest that she could carry her own bag, but then didn't.

When they arrived at the stand and had plunked down their bags of apples, Nick suddenly reached into his pocket for his phone. He checked his text, frowning.

"Who's it from?" asked Lindsay, then immediately regretted it. In the old days, she wouldn't have thought twice about asking him. But now they ran in very different social circles.

"Oh, it's, um, well, it's—" Nick stammered.

"Sorry, I shouldn't have asked," Lindsay said quickly. "Really, it's none of my business."

"It was no one," Nick said. "I mean, nothing important." He shoved the phone back into his pocket.

Of course it has to be from Cassidy, Lindsay thought. *Probably saying thanks for the romantic dinner last night.*

"Hayride! Hayride!" yelled Ellie, jumping up and down and pointing across the field, where a small clump of people was getting onto the back of the hay wagon.

"Mommy, can I go with Lindsay and Nick? Please thank you please?"

Marissa smiled. "Ellie has decided if she uses enough magic words, she can get what she wants," she said to Lindsay. Then she turned to Ellie. "If it's okay with Lindsay and Nick, then sure," she said. "Maybe the grown-ups will go into the barn and have a cup of hot cider."

Ellie shoved her sticky hands into Lindsay's and Nick's and pulled them toward the hayride station. They both allowed her to drag them.

The line had grown longer as more people emerged from the orchard, and the three of them were at the very end. Ellie kept the conversation going as she prattled on about what she was doing in school, and what she was going to be for Halloween, and how she was going to go shopping for new sneakers tomorrow. By the time the hay wagon pulled up, the awkwardness caused by the text Nick received had passed, and things were more or less back to normal.

Everyone was climbing onto the wagon, but when the three of them got to the front of the line, the young guy manning the line stopped them.

"Real sorry," he said, "but I only have room for two

more on here, and it's the last run of the day."

"That's fine," said Nick and Lindsay quickly and at exactly the same time.

"He can go."

"She can go."

Again they spoke at the same time.

"Awwwww!" said Ellie, looking devastated. "I want to go with you both! Please, yes, please, nice man? Can we all go together?"

The man grinned down at her. "Tell you what," he said. "My brother Sam is heading here now in the pickup. I recognize you guys. You come every year. Since you're such loyal customers, I'll have him give you your own special hayride, just the three of you, okay?"

Ellie squealed with delight. The guy sent a quick text to his brother, and then he was off with the hay wagon.

Nick rolled his eyes and nudged Lindsay. "That kid has it all figured out. She charms everyone into saying yes to her."

Lindsay laughed. "It's because she's so cute."

Two minutes later, Sam showed up in the pickup. "Hop in, guys!" he said cheerfully. "Hope you don't mind my dog, Monty. He loves little kids."

Ellie was already clambering over the tailgate of the truck to join Monty, who was waiting expectantly, his tail wagging back and forth.

Nick and Lindsay exchanged glances and climbed on after Ellie.

The truck had a layer of hay bales on it, so there were comfy seats.

"I'm sitting next to Monty!" announced Ellie, who had taken a seat next to the dog. She threw her arms around him, and Monty began licking her ear, making Ellie giggle.

Nick and Lindsay sat side-by-side on a hay bale near the rear.

"Here's a blanket for you guys," said Sam, tossing them a rolled woolen blanket. It landed neatly at their feet. "It's getting colder out, so get cozy."

Lindsay flushed with embarrassment, but she leaned down and unrolled the blanket. She was glad to have it, now that the sun was getting lower in the sky and the wind was picking up. Ellie was all bundled up in her lavender hooded parka and didn't seem to mind the wind a bit.

The truck started moving slowly.

"Hey, let me have some of that blanket too, blanket hog," said Nick playfully, moving closer to Lindsay and tucking a corner of the blanket around himself.

Lindsay grinned. As they rode ever so slowly along the bumpy edge of the field, her mind began to whirl. She'd been this close to Nick about a million times in her life, but now it felt so different. Every time his long leg brushed against hers, it was as though she'd been jolted with electricity. But in a good way. Then they went over a bump, and she felt his shoulder touch hers. Another jolt.

Was he still that mad at her? Was she, for that matter, still mad at him? From the way they were sitting, it didn't feel at all like two people who were mad at each other. It was so confusing.

She might as well get it out in the open. Make it like old times. Like when they used to be able to talk to each other about anything.

"So," she said, her voice coming out a little too high. "Are you, um, going out with Cassidy? That's what everyone is saying. It's fine if you are. Obviously. It's not like I care or anything like that. I just wondered." Her words came out in a big rush.

Nick hesitated. "Well, see, here's the situation," he said, as though measuring his words carefully. "I'm—"

His phone buzzed again. He checked the message,

sighed, and shoved it back into his pocket.

Lindsay pulled the blanket more closely around herself, feeling a new chill. Why did it annoy her so much when he got texts? He was allowed to get them.

He cleared his throat and turned to look at her. "Okay, so you know the harvest dance that's happening in two weeks?"

Lindsay nodded quickly, bracing herself. He was going to tell her he was taking Cassidy, of course. She could deal with that. It's not like it was a huge surprise.

"Well, Troy Lewis has been texting me all day. He wants to know if you want to go. With him. To the dance."

LINDSAY'S JAW DROPPED OPEN. SHE CLOSED IT quickly. That was the last thing she'd expected Nick to say.

"I guess he likes you and wants to ask you out or whatever."

What was it about that name that rang a bell? She couldn't think where she'd heard it. "Troy Lewis? Do I even know him?" was all she could stammer out.

He shrugged. "He knows you. He and I are on the soccer team together. He's in eighth grade. Tall kid? Plays sweeper? Good left foot?" He looked at her and shrugged. "Never mind. I forgot you never come to my games."

"You've only had one so far, plus the tournament," said Lindsay a little defensively. "I'm planning to come to your next home game."

"Well, whatever. Anyway, Troy and I were at soccer

camp together this summer, so we kind of got to know each other. He found out you and I were, well, were friends, so he asked me to ask you."

Suddenly she remembered why that name was familiar to her. Troy. That was the guy Rosie had a crush on, wasn't it? Obviously Lindsay wasn't interested in going to the dance with him, especially if it was going to upset Rosie. But she had to admit, it was pretty flattering that an older guy, a really popular jock older guy, would be interested in her.

"Wow, that's kind of cool!" she said, grinning. "It's not every day you get asked out by a popular eighth-grade guy."

Nick smiled tightly. "Yeah. Cool. How 'bout that."

"But I barely know who he is. Why would he want to go with *me*?" Her voice came out all giddy-sounding.

"Because you're—" Nick stopped and closed his mouth. "He just does, is all. So what should I say to him? Should I tell him no? That you don't even know who he is?"

"No!" said Lindsay quickly. "I mean, no, don't say no. And don't tell him I don't know who he is. I mean, now that you mention him, I do kind of know who he is. He's pretty cute."

Nick waited. A muscle in his cheek twitched.

Lindsay sat back, intrigued. Obviously she didn't like Troy, because she barely knew who he was. And, of course, there was the fact that her best friend had a crush on him already, so there was no way Lindsay could even really consider him in that way. And didn't she really want Nick to ask her? *Oh,* she thought. Did she? She knew she didn't want Nick to go with Cassidy. But did she want Nick to go with her? All this was so confusing. But it was pretty awesome to have a popular eighth-grade boy interested in her.

And if she was being really honest with herself, Lindsay had to admit that it was satisfying to be able to show Nick that he wasn't the only kid at Central Falls Middle School who was All That. She, Lindsay, had popular guys interested in *her*, too.

"Okay, so don't say anything to him yet," said Lindsay. "I need to think about it." A smile tugged at the corners of her mouth.

"What's to think about?" said Nick, his eyes flashing. "Either you like the guy or you don't."

Lindsay looked at him in surprise. He had some nerve, when he hadn't even bothered to tell her he was taking Cassidy to the dance. What right did he have to be so judgmental about her?

The truck slowed to a stop. She hadn't even noticed they were back where they'd started, and that the parents were all standing there waiting for them. She and Nick climbed out in silence.

The car ride home was awkward. Nick had grown moody. Ellie fell asleep almost immediately, a half-eaten apple in her hand. Lindsay delicately extracted it from her grip and placed it in the drink cup next to her, and then stared out the window, lost in thought. On his side of the car, Nick was busy with his phone, checking sports scores while alternately texting back and forth with someone, probably Cassidy.

When Lindsay got home, she went straight to the piano and played stormy, agitated music for a while, ignoring the dynamics and playing the chords triple forte the whole way through. Playing music to suit her mood always seemed to make her feel better, and it did this time. She closed the lid and then sat down at the computer. She'd barely logged in when Rosie sent her an IM.

Where have u been all day?

Went apple picking today with Nick and his family. Can you say 'awkward'?

You know how many girls from school wish they were you?

Yeah, whatever. He may suddenly be Mr. Hot but I think he must have had a brain transplant over the summer ha ha.

Ha ha LOL

Was Cassidy her usual charming self at the tournament yesterday?

Ugh. She barely even makes conversation with seventh graders now, except for NL of course. I heard her talking to Corinne on the bus about the dress she wants to wear to the harvest dance. She saw it in some catalog and she was talking about how great the color would look with her hair—makes me gag.

Ha ha

> She's really spoiled. Her parents must let her buy whatever clothes she wants. And she's traveled to really fancy places. She even went to Europe last summer with her fancy soccer team.

Lindsay tapped her lower lip and thought about the best way to feel out Rosie on the subject of Troy Lewis.

> So who do you like?

> You know. TL, remember? He scored two goals yesterday even though he plays sweeper. He is so awesome!

> Awesome. Oops, got to go. ttyl!

That settled it. She had to let Troy know ASAP that she couldn't go to the dance with him.

Drumming her fingers on the desk, Lindsay thought about it a little more. On the other hand, it was kind of fun to see Nick a little steamed up about it. Obviously he wasn't jealous, because he didn't think of Lindsay *that way*. But for whatever reason, he seemed not to be that psyched about the fact that Troy wanted her to go to the dance with him.

Maybe she wouldn't tell Troy no right away. What was the harm in waiting a little bit? It's not like Rosie would find out that he wanted to ask her. Rosie didn't even know him, really. Maybe she could get Nick to see her and Troy together just once or twice before she turned him down. And to further annoy Nick, she would ask him for Troy's cell phone number. She wouldn't tell him why she wanted it. Let him wonder.

She texted Nick and asked him. He didn't respond.

With a sigh she put down her phone and went upstairs to do her homework. Her All About Me project was mostly done, but she had several subjects to go.

An hour later her phone buzzed. It was a text from Nick.

It was a phone number and nothing else. No *hey, here you go,* or *it was fun today* or anything. Just the number, which she assumed was Troy's. She didn't respond to Nick.

She typed a message to Troy, wording it carefully so she didn't appear too pushy or too flirty—just friendly.

Hey what's up. Heard you guys played great yesterday.

Almost immediately, she got a response from Troy.

Yeah we did pretty well ha ha.

That's awesome well c u tomorrow at school maybe. g2g

Ok c u.

She clicked off her phone and smiled. Flirting was kind of fun. But she would keep it casual like that and not let things progress too far. She would never break Rosie's heart by actually saying yes to Troy for the dance. But maybe just a little more flirting—next time in front of Nick—wouldn't do any harm.

Her phone buzzed, causing her to jump. But it was just Rosie calling.

"Hey," Lindsay said cautiously. Had Rosie somehow heard about Troy? Her stomach felt like she'd swallowed a coiled spring.

"Hey," said Rosie. "There's something awkward I need to tell you."

Lindsay swallowed. "Oh . . . kaaaaay," she said. "What's up?"

"Well you know how you and I said we might maybe hang out together this Friday night? Well, now I can't. Because, see, there's this party? On Friday? And the awkward thing is, I don't think you're invited and I didn't want you to find out and be upset."

The spring in her stomach uncoiled, but only partly. All thoughts of Troy vanished from Lindsay's mind. "Oh. Okay. Thanks for telling me," she said. Her mind was roiling. Had she done something really terrible she wasn't even aware of? Was the whole grade mad at her for some reason?

"See, it's a soccer team party. Sort of," said Rosie quickly. "But see, it's . . . it's at Cassidy's house. And she's invited the girls' team and the boys' team so for sure Corrine and Ava and I will be there, but I heard that a few of her other nonsoccer friends are also invited. And I guess her house is really fancy and they're going to cater it with real waiters and they've got a DJ and dancing and she has a huge pool that's heated so we'll be able to go swimming even if it's cold." She stopped, perhaps thinking she'd shared a little too much information. "Anyway, I just felt bad that you might find out about it and wonder why I was going."

"That's fine. Thanks for telling me, Rosie." Lindsay spoke the words with effort, but she forced her voice to sound casual, unconcerned.

"Oh, good, so you're not mad?" Rosie sounded relieved.

"No, of course I'm not mad. Why should I be mad?" lied Lindsay. "Oops, gotta go, my mom's calling me. See you tomorrow."

"Bye."

She clicked off and just sat there quietly, but her lips quivered a little. Who cared? Who cared if Cassidy was having some big party that sounded like it would be extremely fun, and that Nick would be there, and that Rosie was going, and Ava and Corrine for sure, and probably also Sasha and Bella and Chloe and Jenn, because they were really popular but she wasn't? Was it the end of the world that she wasn't invited?

Kind of.

THE SECOND WEEK OF SCHOOL HAD NONE OF THE excitement and novelty of the first week, and twice the homework. For the first few days, Lindsay avoided Nick as best she could. Luckily they only had homeroom and lunch together. A few times she overheard kids talking about Cassidy's party, but she tried not to pay attention. So what if there was a big party for mostly the soccer players? She didn't even like soccer very much. She knew that Rosie was trying to be sensitive and to shush people up when she drew close, and while she appreciated Rosie's effort, it didn't help much. It really stunk to be excluded. Because Troy was an eighth grader, she had no classes with him, and on Monday, Tuesday, and Wednesday, she saw Troy only in the lunchroom. The first time, at lunch on Monday, she barely registered who he was until he had passed by with his tray, and then she kicked herself for not saying hi. He hadn't even looked her way, though. She wondered if Nick had been playing a mean trick on her or something. What if it was all a hoax? What if Troy had never even said that to Nick about wanting to ask her to the dance? She dismissed that. Nick might have turned stuck-up, but he wasn't mean. He wouldn't set her up for humiliation like that.

The second time she saw Troy, at lunch on Tuesday, she was standing next to Rosie and didn't even see him coming, until Rosie drew in her breath sharply and clutched Lindsay's arm so tightly Lindsay almost dropped her tray. Then she realized what was happening. The two girls stood stock still as Troy passed by with a group of eighth-grade boys.

This time he looked up as he passed by and jerked his chin up, by way of greeting. "'Sup," he said in their general direction, not looking directly at either girl, and kept going.

"He said hello!" squealed Rosie in Lindsay's ear. "And here I thought he didn't even know I was alive!"

Lindsay shifted uncomfortably. Maybe she should tell Rosie about Troy and how he might possibly be asking Lindsay to the dance but that she planned to say no.

No, she couldn't do that. What if Rosie thought she was doing it just to get back at her about the party? She really didn't blame Rosie for wanting to go, but maybe Rosie would think she did. Plus, he hadn't actually asked her. It wasn't really an issue yet. She'd wait and see what happened.

On the way to social studies on Tuesday afternoon, Cassidy stopped Lindsay in the hallway. She looked amazing with her glossy hair bouncing around her shoulders. She had on a perfectly cut white T-shirt, jeans, and a thick belt. Lindsay was pretty sure the T-shirt hadn't come out of Cassidy's dad's drawer. It was probably designer.

"Hey, Lindsay, Corrine told me she heard that you are an awesome piano player," said Cassidy. "Is that true?"

Lindsay narrowed her eyes. Was Cassidy making fun of her? Being a classical musician just wasn't something really popular kids did, and Lindsay and Cassidy both knew it. All the band kids sat together at lunch, and even though some were really nice, and a few were really smart, they were just hopelessly unpopular. Was Cassidy about to ask her why she didn't sit with them at lunch?

"Yeah, I guess," she said with a shrug.

"That's so cool. I wish I could play," said Cassidy. "Guess I'll stick to soccer, though," she added. "The guys are way cuter than the ones in the band!" She giggled and kept moving.

Lindsay wanted to call after her to tell her that piano wasn't even a band instrument, but she thought better of it. Why start another conversation with her when Cassidy would probably just turn it into a reminder of how she got to spend all her time with Nick, and Lindsay didn't? Lindsay was cranky. Why was Cassidy asking her about piano anyway? Did she want to know if Nick liked piano?

That Thursday Lindsay found the perfect opportunity to be seen with Troy in sight of Nick.

The boys' team had a game across town against their biggest rivals. She knew they'd all be assembling at the end of the parking lot closest to the gym. She worked out the whole "chance encounter," even going to her locker before last period to collect her stuff so she wouldn't have to take the time after the bell rang at the end of the day.

That gave her a full seven or eight minutes to happen to pass by the boys' team before her bus left. They'd been excused five minutes early, so she knew they'd be there.

She dashed toward the hallway leading to the gym, heading down the stairs and out that exit door. Sure enough, there were the boys, standing around in their uniforms, joking and laughing with one another. She spotted Troy right away. He was teaching some new soccer kick to Nick. She slowed down and caught her breath, and then walked slowly and casually past the boys toward where the buses were lining up.

Troy saw her and stopped demonstrating whatever kick he'd been showing Nick. He said something to Nick and trotted across the grass toward her. She pretended not to see him.

"Hey," he said.

"Oh! Hi!" she said, pretending to be surprised. "I had to, um, do something at the gym so I came out that way. Looks like you guys have a game today. Who are you playing?"

"We play Crosby. They're good but we can beat them."

"Oh! Well, good luck. Guess I should hustle off to my bus."

Out of the corner of her eye, she could see that Nick had moved over to another clump of his teammates. He was standing next to them quietly, not participating in their conversation. He looked annoyed. Good.

"Hey, hold up a second," said Troy.

She stopped. Oh no. Her heart thumped as she realized he was going to ask her to the dance.

"I was just wondering. You know the harvest dance coming up?"

Think, think, think, she said to herself, feeling panicky. "Oh, yeah, I know, I heard about it!" she said, speaking quickly. "It sounds like it's going to be really fun but I can't go which is really too bad but anyway I have to get to my bus I think it's about to leave good luck in your game hope you win see you bye!" She just had time to note the look of confusion that registered on Troy's face before she turned and trotted in the direction of the throngs of kids at the other end of the parking lot.

She was the last one onto the bus, and there were almost no seats left.

There was one, though. Right next to David Costello. He was sitting toward the front, with the other uncool sixth graders. When he saw her get on, he immediately scooted over to the window so she could sit down. Of all the people to see at a time like this.

She said hello quickly, and then sank down into the seat and breathed out a long sigh. That had been awkward. She hadn't expected Troy to ask her so quickly. All she'd meant to do was to let Nick see her flirting with him, just so Nick would realize how obnoxious *he* looked, flirting with Cassidy.

The question was, would Troy tell Nick that he'd asked her and that she'd turned him down? Well, she hadn't exactly given him a chance to ask her. Maybe Troy wouldn't mention anything to Nick.

She wondered if she should tell Rosie about the whole thing. But Rosie would definitely get upset. And the last thing Lindsay wanted to do was to upset Rosie. She was beginning to regret that she hadn't just told Rosie the truth from the beginning. She hated having a secret from her. The odds were against Rosie even finding out, but still . . . Lindsay felt like she had handled the whole situation the wrong way.

"Boo."

She turned. David Costello was grinning at her with those big purple braces. As her eyes moved past the braces, she noticed for the first time that David's eyes were a startling shade of blue and rimmed with thick, dark lashes.

"You're awfully thoughtful this afternoon," he said in that loud voice of his.

"It's complicated," Lindsay replied, not really in the mood to chat. Hopefully David would get the hint.

Or not. "Saw you talking to that soccer dude, what's-his-name, just now. You do lead an exciting life, don't you?"

She frowned. "Sometimes it's a little too exciting."

"Hey, I have this really cool duet. You want to try playing it sometime?" He pulled a slim music volume from the backpack at his feet and showed it to her.

"'Concertino in E-flat major for piano and clarinet,'" read Lindsay. She shook her head and pushed it back toward him. "I don't think so, thanks."

"It's a great piece," he persisted. "And don't worry, it's not like I'm suggesting it because I 'like' you," he said, using air quotes.

"Oh, well, *that's* a relief," she said, smiling a little. What was that word again that her dad would use to describe this kid? *Cheeky.* David Costello was definitely cheeky.

"Yeah, you're not really my type. Plus, I have my eye on someone else," he continued, nodding contentedly.

"A seventh grader. She's gorgeous."

Lindsay suppressed her urge to giggle. Where did this kid get all that confidence? He was short. He had purple braces. Still, there was something kind of charming about him. He was comfortable in his own skin. He was easy to talk to, almost like the way Nick used to be easy to talk to.

"Listen, thanks anyway," she said, "but my social life is complicated enough right now. I don't really need to further damage my already-damaged reputation by being seen in the band room practicing some dorky music—no offense."

He shrugged. "Suit yourself."

He didn't seem offended by what she'd said, which, upon reflection, she felt a little bad about. She'd been a bit harsh, calling it dorky music, she had to admit. But the kid had a thick skin. He stood up as the bus's brakes screeched. "This is my stop. See ya."

chapter 10

THAT EVENING LINDSAY RAN THROUGH HER ALL About Me presentation several times. She was dreading it. Why did it have to be first thing in the morning? And why did they have to present it? Couldn't they just write a report like they usually did? She was really different from her older brother, who loved to perform—on stage, at a party, wherever. Some people were just like that, but not her.

She flicked through the slides on her computer, frowning.

Several kids had already presented over the course of that week, and their presentations had been really interesting, she had to admit. She had had no idea that Nadia Melek's father had been born in Cairo, or that Nadia spoke Arabic. Before the presentation, Lindsay thought people in Egypt spoke Egyptian.

She had been amazed to learn that Ned Norman had won a robotics competition when he was ten, and that he'd already placed out of tenth-grade math.

Claudia Flores, the Mexican exchange student, had shown them pictures of the town she was from in Mexico, and each one looked like a postcard. There were candy-colored buildings bathed in sunlight; azure, glimmering beaches; and her village square at night, with sparkly lights and outdoor restaurants, where people milled around all dressed up. Lindsay couldn't imagine leaving a place that pretty and coming to live here. Claudia showed a picture of her with her three brothers. One of her brothers had even played for the Mexican national soccer team. Nick let out a "Whoa, no way!" when Claudia told them that. Lindsay turned off her computer and opened her math book, staring down at the problems and frowning.

The fact that the other kids' presentations had gone so well just made Lindsay feel worse, not better, about her own presentation. Those kids were interesting. They had real stories to tell. Hers was going to be so dull. What was so interesting about her family? A mom who used to be a concert pianist but was now just a mom who taught piano lessons on the side. A dad who was a lawyer, and not the rich kind. A brainiac brother who was better at piano than she was, and also really good-looking and theatrical, off at college. Big yawn. Claudia's brother played on a *professional* soccer team. Ned Norman was not only a genius, but he also had a really cool family—one of his uncles was a police detective in New York City.

She closed her math book with a sigh. There was no way she could concentrate on it when she was all stressed about the presentation. She'd do her math in study hall tomorrow. She lay back on her bed and stared at the ceiling.

And to make it even more awkward? Even though she edited as many out as she could, a full two-thirds of the pictures in her slide show featured Nick. And Cassidy would be sitting right in front of her, probably snickering her head off, gloating about going out with Nick and thinking how Lame Lindsay thought they were still friends. Things really couldn't get much worse.

Except that they could.

That night she tossed and turned a lot, fretting about her presentation, about Nick, about anything and everything, the way you only do in the middle of the night. At last, toward morning, she managed to doze off. When her alarm went off, she was tired but somehow she also felt a new resolve.

She was not going to worry about what people

thought. She would give her presentation, and everyone could just deal with it.

It was true, wasn't it, that she and Nick had grown up together? That they had been best friends for nearly thirteen years? She had thirteen years' worth of pictures to prove it. And she wasn't going to deny her past. Sure, he'd changed. He was different. But that was now. This was then. What he'd become didn't change who he had once been.

She chose her outfit carefully. She didn't want to look too dressed up, or like she'd fussed too much. It was too warm for her favorite red sweater, and anyway, she'd worn that apple picking. She finally decided on her second-favorite top, a blouse that buttoned up the front and was gathered in a little at the waist, and her second-favorite pair of pants, her raspberry-colored corduroys. She put on some strawberry lip gloss and gathered her hair in a ponytail, then looked in the mirror. It was fine. She looked okay. She was not glamorous like Cassidy, and never would be, but she looked like herself: a sort-of pretty, smart, fringe-popular girl.

At school, she got to homeroom early, but stood outside the door, gathering her courage. This would be no big deal. She wished she didn't get so nervous speaking in front of a group, but she would handle it just fine.

Cassidy appeared and shimmied sideways past her to get into the room. "Hi, Lindsay," she said. "You're presenting today, right?"

"Yep."

"I think it's so cool that you didn't get all dressed up and whatever! I'm totally stressing about what to wear for my presentation, but it's neat that you don't care!" said Cassidy in a sweet voice, and then she disappeared into the classroom.

Before she could react to that, Lindsay's phone vibrated in her pocket. She looked around quickly. Who would be texting her now? She could get in trouble if she got caught using her phone, but this had to be important. She pulled it half out of her pocket and peeked at the screen.

It was from Rosie. Lindsay slipped out her phone and looked at it, hidden behind her note cards.

OMG Linz I am SO SORRY!!!

Lindsay gulped, then quickly texted back.

For what???!!

There followed a long pause. The first bell rang. That meant she had only three minutes or so before the second bell rang. She didn't know what Mr. Bates would do if she was tardy on the day she was supposed to present! At last her phone vibrated again and then once more as Rosie replied to her in a series of texts, one after the other.

I mentioned something to Ava at soccer practice yesterday that you and Nick had hung out and had an apple orchard date last weekend. I guess Ava told Bella, and Bella told EVERYONE because this morning Jenn texted me and said everyone is talking about it.

Before Lindsay could text a reply, another message came through.

And Jenn heard that some kids are saying that you have been telling everyone that you and Nick are going out now. They heard you ask him out in the hallway!!

What????!!!!

Sorry, bell's going to ring. g2g see u at lunch. Sorrryyyyyy!!!

Lindsay shoved her phone back into her pocket and stood there in a daze. The second bell rang, which snapped her out of it. She hurried into class and was in her seat before the bell had stopped ringing.

She looked up, trying to catch Nick's eye, but he would not look in her direction. He had heard the rumors for sure. She darted a glance at Cassidy. Cassidy smiled at her, but Lindsay was sure it was an Evil Smile. Like she was planning to enjoy watching Lindsay crash and burn up there.

Lindsay felt her face get hot all the way up to the roots of her hair. Everyone thought she was this delusional girl who believed she and Nick were boyfriend and girlfriend, and was going around declaring that to be true, even though he was obviously going out with Cassidy. And now she had to get up there and do a presentation that was basically a Me and Nick show? That would confirm every one of the rumors. They'd think she was a stalker with a huge, one-sided crush on Nick.

There was no way she could go through with it. Maybe she could will herself to faint on the spot. She tried but it didn't work. She remained fully conscious.

"Lindsay Potter? Are you all set to present?" called Mr. Bates.

Nick looked up and met her eye. She couldn't read his expression. Was he mad? Upset? Did he feel sorry for her?

She opened her mouth to say something and then closed it again.

The clock ticked.

Someone coughed.

A chair scraped.

Mr. Bates raised his eyebrows encouragingly.

Cassidy moved her chair a couple of inches closer to Nick's, and crossed her arms expectantly.

That made Lindsay mad.

She'd do it anyway, no matter what rumors were flying around. Cassidy might get to say she and Nick were going out if she wanted to. But she, Lindsay, knew him better than anyone. Practically better than his own mom. People could think what they wanted to think. If people wanted to believe the rumors, there wasn't much she could do about that.

She stood up and walked to the front of the room, feeling her face burning. With shaking hands, she stuck her flash drive into the port on the classroom computer. She looked up quickly. Claudia Flores was smiling at her in a sweet way, as if to say she'd been there and knew how Lindsay must be feeling. That helped. Lindsay smiled back gratefully.

She clicked on her first slide. It was a picture of her mom, hugely pregnant, standing belly to belly with Marissa, also hugely pregnant. The class tittered.

After introducing herself, she started in. "This is my mom. And this is her best friend, Marissa. She and Marissa were pregnant at almost the exact same time. They had babies five days apart. I was born on March fifth. Marissa's baby was born on March tenth." She paused. "Marissa named her baby Nick." She paused. "As in, Nick Lopez."

The class erupted in surprise. Mr. Bates shushed them, but he, too, was looking fascinated. Nick grinned uncomfortably and readjusted his long legs to the other side of his desk.

She clicked to the next slide. "This is me at one day old. That boy is my older brother, Matthew. He was six when I was born."

"Awwww," some of the girls said.

Matthew was grinning ear to ear as he held his baby sister in his arms and beamed at the camera. He had a sprinkle of freckles across his nose, and one of his front teeth was missing. Lindsay paused. Matthew was kind of a cute kid, she realized.

The next few slides were pictures of Lindsay's family, her grandparents, a piano recital poster showing her very young-looking mother looking very glamorous in a long black gown. She showed a picture of her dad with a lot more hair on his head, back when he graduated from law school. The kids were polite as she talked, if a bit fidgety.

But then she clicked to the next slide. It was a picture of two babies sitting with their backs to the camera on the piano bench and slamming on the keys, turned partly toward the person taking the picture, giggling. "The fat one is Nick," said Lindsay. Everyone started laughing. Baby Nick was wearing just a diaper, and he really was chubby, the rolls of fat spilling over the top of his diaper, his pudgy wrists like twisted balloons. "He never got much better at piano than that," she added. Big laugh from the class.

Across from Lindsay, Nick sat with his long legs

sprawled under his desk. He wore that half smile on his face, as though he didn't mind the good-natured teasing he was getting, although the tips of his ears had gone red. Was she embarrassing him? Oh well.

And then she flicked through picture after picture of her and Nick—dressed for Halloween as a knight and a princess; on the town soccer team in identical uniforms, when Lindsay had been a full two inches taller than Nick (more laughs); and then at her tenth birthday party, when her dad had taken the two of them, plus Matthew, to a professional baseball game. She and Nick were both dressed in head-to-toe Cubs uniforms. And Lindsay was *still* taller than Nick. Which earned him even more friendly teasing from a few of his friends in the homeroom.

Finally she got to the last slide, a picture of herself from the past summer that her mom had snapped with her smartphone. It showed Lindsay standing in front of their car, clutching a pile of piano books to her chest, grinning widely because she'd just gotten her braces off. She clicked off the projector.

She'd prepared her conclusion and practiced it ten times the night before, but now she addressed the class without looking at her cards. She felt the words bubble up inside her and decided just to say them.

"So now we're in seventh grade," she said. "I think seventh grade is kind of a crossroads. It's time to grow and change and meet new people. We can't necessarily remain friends with people we've known all our lives, because people change." She paused, panicked, and looked down at her card. But she couldn't read it, because her eyes had gotten all misted up. So she just ended with a lame-sounding "So, yeah. That's my presentation," then walked quickly back to her desk and sat down.

Sasha and Jenn both patted her on the arm from either side, whispering that she'd been awesome.

People clapped politely, and Mr. Bates told her "Good job," and then the bell rang and everyone stood up, shouldering backpacks, shuffling papers, and getting ready to head to the first class.

Lindsay shot up from her desk and was one of the first people out of the classroom when the bell rang. She headed straight for the girls' bathroom and into one of the stalls. Once inside, she burst into tears.

chapter 11

SHE COMPOSED HERSELF QUICKLY, THOUGH. Lindsay wasn't even sure why she was so emotional. The talk had gone pretty well, considering. Maybe everyone was gossiping about her "Nick fixation," but there wasn't much she could do about that. She'd found Nick's expressions impossible to read. Was he mad at her? Pleased to be so featured in her presentation? Did he even care? That was probably the worst option, for him to not even care.

She made it to her next class on time and tried to concentrate on school all the way up until lunch. She was dying to see Rosie, to talk to her about everything, about how complicated it all was.

When she got to her locker just before lunch, Rosie was waiting for her. Lindsay took one look at her friend, and her day went from bad to worse. She did not like the look on Rosie's face. It looked mad, and reproachful, and . . . she couldn't say what else.

"Hi," Lindsay said.

Rosie didn't say hi back. She waited until Lindsay was close enough to talk to without other people hearing.

"How come you didn't say anything?" she asked, a glint of a tear in the corner of one eye.

"*What?* Say anything about what?" asked Lindsay quickly, but already dread was creeping through her.

"About Troy? About how you totally were flirting with him? Like about seventeen people said you were. I thought you said you didn't even know who he was!" she said accusingly.

"Rosie, I know it looks bad. But I can explain—I'm really sorry," said Lindsay. "I, well, I heard he was thinking of asking me to the dance, see, but I swear I'm not going with him! I told him no! I didn't want you to be mad!" Everything was coming out all wrong. Her words sounded so lame, so, well, guilt-ridden.

Rosie's face darkened. "You know, Linz, I just don't know what to think right now," she said. "First I hear all these rumors that you've been chasing Nick down the hall and asking him to the dance—"

"That is so not true and you know it!" said Lindsay, her temper flaring. "You're the one who started the rumor that I liked him in the first place!"

Rosie shook her head slowly. "And now you're going around saying that you could have gone to the dance with Troy, but you turned him down?"

"I'm not 'going around saying it,'" retorted Lindsay. "I'm saying it to you." A sick feeling rose up in her, like when you're on a roller coaster that's slowly getting to the top of a huge rise and you know you're about to go flying down on the other side of it and you can't do anything to stop it. She wanted to stop this bad conversation with her friend, but she didn't feel like she could control where it was going. "I just heard he was going to ask me, and I knew you'd be upset, so I said I wasn't going."

"Well, you were right about me being upset," said Rosie, and her dark eyes flashed. "And what I don't get is why you were hanging around him in the first place, after you told me you barely knew him. Now I feel like I barely know you, Lindsay! And that's a pretty rotten way to feel about someone who is supposed to be one of your best friends. Anyway, whatever. I'm going to lunch. I'm starved."

After Rosie left, Lindsay leaned back against the lockers and closed her eyes. She tried to make time move backward, to somehow erase and rerecord the conversation they just had. But she couldn't. Slowly, her feet carried her toward the cafeteria.

Rosie was already at their usual table, but the usual space next to her, where Lindsay always sat, didn't have a chair. There was no place for her to sit. None of her friends looked up, or called to her, or waved her over as they usually did. They were all sitting quietly with their heads down, not talking much to one another.

She looked over at Nick's table. He was sitting with his usual throng of seventh and eighth graders. It was a much livelier, chattier table than the one where Lindsay's friends were sitting, although Nick and Cassidy were sitting with their heads bowed together as though they were having a private conversation.

Panic welled up in her. Should she just go hide in the bathroom until lunch was over? She didn't want to get demerit points for skipping lunch. Plus she was starving. She'd barely touched her breakfast this morning because she'd been so nervous about her presentation.

Without looking around, she collected her tray and

utensils and got her lunch. Then she turned and headed purposefully toward the table where Claudia was sitting, eating more or less by herself, slightly apart from the clump of other kids at the end of the table.

"Mind if I sit with you?" asked Lindsay.

Claudia smiled sweetly and moved her tray a little to allow Lindsay to sit down. "Of course. Please sit!" she said.

Lindsay sat. She liked the way Claudia talked. She said "seet," instead of "sit."

"I enjoyed your talk this morning," said Claudia. "It was so entertaining."

"Thanks," said Lindsay. "I thought yours was really interesting too." She took a tiny bite of macaroni and cheese and tried to swallow past the big lump in her throat. "Are you homesick for Mexico?"

"A little," said Claudia. "But it's nice here, too."

"Do you have brothers and sisters?"

"Three brothers. Two older, one younger."

"Oh, right. I remember that from your presentation," said Lindsay. "And they're all really good soccer players, right? Is that what you guys do for fun back in Mexico?"

"We do play a lot," said Claudia. "I love to play soccer.

I got very good, playing against my brothers. And at my school, I play midfielder."

"Oh! Why don't you play for Central Falls's team, then?" asked Lindsay.

Claudia shook her head wistfully. "I did not bring my soccer shoes—how do you say them, with the bumps underneath?"

"Cleats?"

"Yes, the cleats. And also, my host family has two younger children, only in third and fifth grade. I don't like to ask them to drive me to places."

Lindsay was thoughtful as she picked at her fruit cup. "Yeah, I can see why that might be hard," she said.

"The bell is going to ring in a moment," said Claudia, collecting the paper stuff from around her tray. "I must go try to understand my book for English class. I have read the chapter twice, but it is not easy still. It was very nice to talk with you."

Lindsay smiled, even though she had that huge, annoying lump in her throat. "It was nice to talk to you, too. I'll see you in social studies."

chapter 12

LINDSAY SOMEHOW MANAGED TO GET THROUGH the rest of the day without crying publicly, but it took all her power not to. She saw Rosie in English class, but Rosie didn't even look at her. Even Sasha and Jenn and Chloe were a little standoffish, saying hi to her quickly in the hallway and hurrying on.

She thought miserably about the party at Cassidy's that would be going on that night, the one she hadn't been invited to. What would everyone be saying about her? Would anyone come to her defense if kids started saying mean things about her? In a way, she was glad she wasn't going. She could just go home and lock herself in her room and ignore everything. Well, at least until Monday.

When she got home from school, she could hear the sound of a little kid playing a simple piece, slowly and with lots of mistakes. Lindsay's mom was often teaching a younger kid when Lindsay got home from school, as they got home earlier than the middle schoolers.

She went into the kitchen to make herself a peanut butter and jelly sandwich, since she'd barely touched her lunch. She heard the little kid leave and was just sitting down to eat when her mother came into the kitchen.

"Oh good, I'm glad you're home," said her mom, giving her a kiss on the top of her head. "How was school?"

Hah, thought Lindsay. *It was only the worst day of my life*. "Great," she said dully.

"That's good. I forgot to tell you this," said her mom, checking on something in the oven. "I volunteered for you to babysit tonight. For pay, of course. Please tell me you don't have plans."

Lindsay was quiet for a minute. Actually, babysitting might be a good thing to do that night. It would keep her from moping around in her bedroom, wondering how much fun all her former friends were having at the world's funnest-sounding party that she hadn't been invited to. And she'd also told Rosie she had plans, so now it wouldn't be a lie.

"No, I don't have plans," she said. "Where am I going to be babysitting?"

"Well, ah, it's more of a mother's helper kind of job," said her mother, resetting the oven timer for ten more minutes. "A bunch of people in Daddy's office are having a potluck dinner, an engagement party for a young lawyer, and quite a few people are bringing their kids. The hostess, Mrs. Elkman, asked Daddy if he knew any babysitters. You can keep an eye on the kids while the grown-ups are having dinner. It'll be outside, mostly, although it may turn cold when the sun sets and you may be inside with them as well."

"Okay," said Lindsay. "What time?"

"We have to leave in . . . half an hour," said her mom. "Daddy's meeting us there. Oh, dear, I'd better run and get dressed!"

An hour later, Lindsay found herself in the massive backyard of a large house across town. She'd barely had time to change into babysitting attire—her most comfy sweatshirt, oldest pair of jeans, and sneakers—before they'd had to run out the door.

There were six little kids, ranging in age from three to seven. Lindsay had always liked little kids, and after she oversaw them all eating dinner, they spent a fun half an hour outside in the backyard, creating huge bubbles with oversize bubble wands, playing beach-ball tag, and drawing pictures on the walkway with colored chalk. When dusk set in and it started to get cold, Mrs. Elkman came outside and suggested that Lindsay take them downstairs to the basement, where there were lots of games to play.

"My own kids are all in college now," said Mrs. Elkman, "but we still have all their games down there!"

When Lindsay got down to the basement with the kids, she was surprised to discover an upright piano in the corner. It was old and battered, but in tune, with no keys missing.

"Play us sumpin, Lih-zy!" said the three-year-old girl, Molly. "Play me the 'Eensy Weensy Spider'!"

Lindsay sat down with Molly on her lap and played it. Immediately the rest of the kids dropped their toys and gathered around the piano, enthralled. She found a beaten-up old songbook inside the bench. She played all their suggestions, and the kids sang along exuberantly to each one. They were in the seventh verse of "The Wheels on the Bus" when she became aware that someone had tiptoed down the basement steps and was standing at the bottom of the stairs, listening.

"Okay, guys, let's take a break," said Lindsay after they'd finished the tenth verse. She swiveled her legs around the piano bench and found herself looking straight at Nick.

Chapter 13

HE WAS THE LAST PERSON IN THE WORLD SHE'D expected to find herself staring at.

"Wait, what? What are you doing here?" she stammered.

He grinned. "Hello to you, too," he said, ambling over to the piano.

"I didn't think . . . I mean I thought . . . how do you even know the Elkmans? This is, like, a work party for my dad's office."

"I know," said Nick. "But Alberto and Mrs. Elkman went to college together and they're old friends, and she knew your mom and dad were good friends with my mom and stepdad, so she invited them to come. And . . . I heard maybe you might be here, so I tagged along."

"But what about your—what about Cassidy's party?" asked Lindsay. "Why aren't you there?"

He shifted uncomfortably, dropping his eyes to the floor. "It's fine. I'll show up a little later. It's actually just a few blocks over from here, so I can walk."

For the first time, Lindsay noticed what he was wearing. A polo shirt. Khaki pants. And his hair looked like he'd combed it. She'd never known him to comb his hair, ever. He'd once confessed to her that he just ran his fingers through it once or twice when he got out of the shower, and forgot about it the rest of the day. But she could definitely tell—he had actually parted his hair, sort of. He looked amazing. Great. He was all dolled up to see Cassidy.

She was suddenly aware of how awful she must look, with her hair in a sloppy ponytail, in her old sweatshirt and jeans. It just hadn't occurred to her that she'd run into anyone she knew.

"Hey, Boy!" said Molly, staring up at Nick. "Are you Lih-zy's boyfwend?"

Lindsay cringed. "No, he's just my friend," she said to Molly.

"Can you be the horsie?" demanded Kyle, who was four. He was pointing up at Nick.

Nick grinned and got down on all fours, allowing Kyle

to climb onto his back. For the next half an hour, Lindsay was able to sit back on the couch and relax, watching Nick horseplay with the kids. He let them jump on him, hang from him, ride on him. He taught them card tricks. He showed them how he could stand on his head, and of course they all had to try, with varying degrees of success.

Finally, to settle them down, Lindsay put in a DVD for them. As the kids sat on the floor in front of the TV, entranced, she and Nick had a chance to sit down side-by-side on the comfy old couch.

Lindsay could feel the tension in the air between them, like a live electric wire she dared not touch. She was dying to ask him what he had thought of her presentation, and what gossip everyone was saying about her, and who was going to be at the party. But she couldn't summon the nerve. Maybe she didn't really want to know.

"I haven't heard you play piano in ages," said Nick, breaking the silence. "You're really good, Linz. You should play in the orchestra or for one of the shows or something."

Lindsay flushed. "Thanks. But you know I hate playing in front of people. Plus I don't really broadcast it much around school. It's not exactly cool to brag about being able to play Chopin."

Nick shrugged. "I think it's really cool. And who cares?"

Lindsay nodded. She was remembering, in a big rush, why she liked Nick so much. He really didn't care if things were cool or not. They sat and watched a scene on the kids' DVD, showing two dogs in love with each other, sharing a plate of spaghetti by the light of a romantic moon. It was just a silly cartoon, but Lindsay felt her cheeks grow red watching it with Nick.

"So I guess you'll be heading off to your party, huh?" said Lindsay finally.

"I guess."

"Why did you even come here?" she asked suddenly. The question came out like more of an accusation, even though Lindsay hadn't meant it to.

"Because I, well, I felt like it," he said, a little defensively.

"Does everyone in the whole school hate me?" she asked in a tiny voice.

He looked at her, baffled. "What are you talking about?"

Did he really not know? "Well, for starters, I didn't even get invited to the party tonight."

He rolled his eyes. "It's a *soccer team* party, Linz," he said patiently. "You don't *play* soccer, remember?"

"Yeah, well, that's not what I heard. I heard that it's way more than a soccer party and that Cassidy invited all the cool kids and I know she's intentionally excluding me because she doesn't like me and—"

"Lindsay, where are you getting all this bogus information?" asked Nick, looking genuinely perplexed. "Cassidy is not excluding you. She likes you."

Once again, Lindsay could feel her temper getting the better of her, and her words spilled out without her feeling like she could control what she was saying. "Oh, yeah, right, as if," she retorted. "She is so stuck-up and mean and you know she was going around spreading rumors about me and—"

"Hey," he said. His face was stony. "You have to stop being so judgmental about stuff you don't know anything about. Cassidy is a really nice person. She's a good soccer player, and, well, you shouldn't always jump to conclusions and think everything is all about you, because it's not always, okay?"

He stood up.

"I gotta go," he mumbled, and headed up the stairs.

chapter 14

LINDSAY WOKE UP THE NEXT MORNING AFTER another rough night's sleep. Her parents were already up and out—her mom had left a note on the kitchen table saying they were running their usual Saturday morning errands. Outside the rain poured down, which was appropriate for the mood she was in.

After eating half a bagel that tasted like sawdust in her mouth, she drifted into the living room and sat down at the piano to play. She played Chopin's Prelude in E Minor, the saddest piece on the planet. Her mother had once told her that Chopin had asked for it to be played at his own funeral. It seemed like an appropriately depressing piece to play this morning, when she was feeling deeply sorry for herself.

She searched through the stack of music for something else sad and depressing to play. Beethoven's

"Moonlight Sonata"—perfect. As she was beginning the slow, haunting arpeggios in the right hand, she heard her mom come in, talking with someone. She kept playing.

"Hey, honey!" said her mom from the doorway of the kitchen. "Sorry to interrupt, but I found someone sitting on our front stoop, waiting to talk to you!"

Nick? Her heart leapt. Had he come to apologize? Could it be?

No, it couldn't. When she turned around, she found David Costello standing next to her mom, grinning his big purple smile.

"Good morning, Lindsay," he said. "My, that's sad music, and you're playing it especially mournfully."

"Um, hi," said Lindsay dubiously. "What are you doing here?"

"Lindsay! That's not polite! David is my old student—one of the most talented musicians I've ever taught!" said her mother, putting a hand on David's shoulder. "He says he has a piece he wants you two to play together for the school recital. A duet. I think that would be fabulous."

"David," said Lindsay, feeling her annoyance level rising. "I thought we talked about this. I thought—"

She was getting the death stare from her mom.

Lindsay sighed. "Okay, bring it over and show it to me," she said through gritted teeth.

Her mom nodded and smiled, and then disappeared into the kitchen.

He came over and sat down at the piano, propping the music up on the stand. It was a little too cozy for the two of them on the bench, so Lindsay scooched out and stood next to him, looking at the music.

"It's for the showpiece recital at school in two weeks," he said by way of explanation. "Mr. Thompson was totally psyched when I told him we were going to play a duet together."

"He was—what? You *told* him we were playing a *duet* even after I told you I didn't *want* to?" Lindsay stared at him in disbelief.

He waved a hand in the air dismissively. "I knew you could be convinced. I've known your mother a long time, and although you are obviously very stubborn and appear to have a quick temper, you're smart and you're a good musician. I knew I could make you come around."

"Well, if you know me so well," said Lindsay, "then you also know that I would never play in public."

Another wave of the hand. "Like I already told you,

you have to get over that. Plus, this will be great for your social standing at Central Falls Middle School, trust me. The kids will be all over it. This will make them forget all about the harvest dance nonsense."

She stared at him, half-furious, half-fascinated.

"Look: It's in G major. One sharp. What could be easier?" He began to play the piano part, smoothly, effortlessly. It was really quite a pretty piece.

"I didn't know you still played," said Lindsay, fascinated in spite of her outrage.

He shrugged. "I can play just about any instrument I set my mind to. But right now, I need to concentrate on clarinet. I believe I mentioned before that I have a crush on a girl in the band? Her name is Tiffany Riggins. She plays oboe and sits two seats away from me. This will definitely get her to pay attention. So you'll be helping out an old friend in the process."

Lindsay surrendered to his infectious, offbeat, way-too-confident charm. "Let me try it," she said gruffly, and sat down next to him, shoving him over on the bench.

She was a good sight reader, and the piece wasn't too difficult. After a few stumbles, she had the first two lines down pretty well.

"Excellent," said David. "Next week I'll bring my clarinet to school and we can try it as a duet. We'll meet after school."

"What if I have something to *do* after school?"

He gave her a mildly disappointed look, exactly the way her mom used to look when Lindsay assured her she'd washed her hands, when her mom knew she hadn't. "Come on. We both know you don't have an after-school activity. It will be a great excuse to hang around and take the late bus. You might even see that soccer stud of yours."

Lindsay's mouth dropped open.

"Make sure you watch your dynamics."

"Yes, sir," she said in her most sarcastic voice. "I hope it will meet with your satisfaction."

"I'm sure you'll be great after a few days of practicing," he said, completely missing—or ignoring—her tone. "And now, a little advice?"

She braced herself for what he might say next. Who was this kid? Where did he get the confidence to dole out advice to her? They hardly knew each other, and he was a mere sixth grader. Didn't he understand his place in the social order of things? She was way more popular than he was, or at least she had been until yesterday.

"Stop being so proud. Stop worrying about what everyone is going to say or think. Just be yourself, because that's all any of us can really be. That's what my grandmother used to tell me, anyway, and you just looked like you could use that advice. Just guessing, of course." David got up from the piano bench. "Well, gotta run. I have a music lesson at the academy in forty minutes. They think I'm a child prodigy." He grinned. "See you at school."

And he walked out, leaving Lindsay staring after him in amazed disbelief.

She spent the next hour practicing her part of the duet.

chapter 15

IT WAS STILL RAINING, BUT LINDSAY MADE THE long walk anyway, not wanting to wait until the weather let up.

Rosie opened the door. She stared at Lindsay, aghast. "Lindsay! What are you doing here, standing in the pouring rain? Come in quick! Are you a nutcase?" She peered outside, looking for a car in the driveway. "Did you walk all the way here from your house? That's like, two miles!"

Lindsay stepped in and set down her dripping umbrella, but did not unzip her raincoat. She didn't want Rosie to think she was assuming she could stay for long. But Rosie insisted she take it off, so she hung it on the doorknob of the hall closet door.

Lindsay peered down the hall toward the kitchen, wondering if Rosie's family was around.

"They're not here," said Rosie in answer. "They all went to the mall. I have to babysit later, so I couldn't go."

Lindsay nodded. "Rosie, I came over to say I'm sorry."

"It's okay, Linz, I—"

"No, but listen. I really need to tell you this. You were right that I went and flirted with Troy. I was awful to pretend to Troy that I liked him. I only did it because I was trying to make Nick jealous. See, I know this won't be a surprise to you because I know everyone's talking about it, but the rumors are true. I really do like Nick. I seem to be the last one on earth to realize it. I didn't even really know I liked him until, well, until I finally admitted to myself that I liked him more than just as a friend. Even though he's going out with Cassidy, and he hates my guts. And it was really lame of me to fake that I was interested to Troy. I feel terrible about it."

"Linz, it's fine. I totally get it. I understand. And anyway I don't even *like* Troy anymore."

"Oh! You—you don't? Did something happen?"

"Yes. I'll tell you what happened. I finally realized—duh!—that Kevin Avery, the striker, is, like, to die for gorgeous." She put a hand to her heart and then fanned herself. "Have you noticed?"

Lindsay smiled, overcome with relief. "No, I hadn't. I guess I should get to a game one of these days."

"Yes, you should," said Rosie. "I really appreciate the apology, Lindsay. I think I kind of overreacted and didn't let you tell me what happened, and I feel bad about it. But it's done, so now let's move on, okay? Come into the kitchen and I'll heat you up a cup of hot cocoa. My mom made it this morning and it is soooooo good."

She linked arms with Lindsay and led her into the kitchen.

Lindsay sat down at the Pereiras' cozy kitchen table, feeling better than she'd felt in days. Rosie turned on the gas burner, which whooshed into flame below the pot of cocoa on the stove. Then she turned it down to low.

"So I have to ask. How was the party last night?" asked Lindsay cautiously.

"It was pretty fun," said Rosie. "There were a lot of kids there but they were mostly all soccer players. Sasha and Jenn and Chloe were not there . . . they weren't invited, it turns out. There was a ton of supervision—like five caterers and a DJ and there was even a *lifeguard* supervising us in the pool."

Lindsay nodded, hoping Rosie would get to talking about Nick and Cassidy.

"And the house was crazy nice," Rosie went on. She ladled some cocoa into a cup and set it down in front of Lindsay.

It smelled amazing. She took a sip. It tasted delicious.

"It belongs to Cassidy's grandparents, I guess. They have a huge pool and a huge backyard and the house is huge with a ginormous kitchen and down in the basement they have a movie theater room and a game room that's better than a lot of arcades I've been to!" Rosie's words were tumbling out. "I guess Cassidy has a ton of cousins so the grandparents decked out the basement for when they all come to visit, but Cassidy said they don't even visit all that often."

"What was her family like?" Lindsay said, no longer pretending she wasn't dying of curiosity.

Rosie furrowed her brow. "I don't think her parents were actually there," she said. "The only one I saw was her grandmother, but she was all dressed up to go out to some fancy party herself. Anyway, it was really fun but I wished you were there."

"Did you see Nick there?"

"Yeah, he showed up late, though," said Rosie.

Of course he did. He'd been with Lindsay at her parents' party, getting mad at her. "Was he, like, hanging out with Cassidy all night?"

Rosie set down the ladle on a plate and turned to look at her. "Not really. He mostly was hanging out with his teammates. I talked to him a little bit. You know what, Linz? I am really glad you came over. But I think you also need to talk to Nick."

Monday morning Lindsay's dad had an early meeting, so he gave her a ride to school. As she headed toward the area near the playground, where kids tended to congregate and socialize before school, the first person she saw was Cassidy.

Should I walk past her and pretend not to see her? wondered Lindsay. But she didn't have the opportunity. Cassidy spotted her, waved, and hurried over.

"Today's my day," she said.

Lindsay looked confused. "For what?" she asked. "Do you have some big game or something?"

"Duh, no. It's my day for the All About Me presentation!"

"Oh!" Lindsay looked surprised. She had been so busy noticing when she herself was going, and when Nick was going, that she'd totally not even noticed that Cassidy was presenting right in between the two of them.

"I ran through it for Nicky on Saturday, and he thought it was pretty good," said Cassidy. "But he's always so nice, who knows if he really meant it."

Again, Lindsay felt the jealousy roil around her, thinking about Nick and Cassidy being so chummy like that. Again with the *Nicky*. And when had they gone through it? Had he gone over to her house after the party? Maybe they'd spent the whole weekend hanging out together.

"Okay, well, good luck with that," said Lindsay, moving on. And then she saw Claudia leaning against the building, looking down at her notebook.

A thought suddenly struck her.

"Can you wait here for one sec?" she asked Cassidy.

Cassidy's perfect eyebrows arched upward in surprise, but she shrugged and nodded.

Lindsay was by Claudia's side a moment later. "Hey, Claudia. Can you, um, come over there with me? I just want you to talk to someone."

Claudia, too, looked surprised, but she nodded and shoved the notebook back into her backpack. Slinging the heavy bag up onto her shoulder, she followed after Lindsay.

"Cassidy, do you know Claudia?" asked Lindsay when the three girls were standing together.

"Um, yeah, hi," said Cassidy. "You're in our homeroom, right? Aren't you from, like, Morocco or something?"

"Mexico," Lindsay and Claudia corrected her at the same time.

"Hello," said Claudia. She looked sideways at Lindsay as though she was wondering where this was going.

"Claudia here is a soccer player," said Lindsay. "And I was thinking maybe she might be able to come to one of your practices? Maybe practice with the team, to see how she plays and stuff? Her brothers are professional soccer players, if you remember from her presentation."

Claudia's eyes widened with surprise, but she didn't say anything.

"Sure!" said Cassidy. "Practice today is at three thirty. I'll tell Coach. I'm sure she won't mind if you practice with us."

"But I do not want my host family to need to drive me too much," said Claudia.

"There's a late bus after practice," said Cassidy. "You just have to sign up at the office."

"And the shoes. I don't have the shoes with the bumps for the soccer."

Lindsay started to explain to Cassidy that Claudia was talking about cleats, but Cassidy was already nodding her head. "What size are you?" she asked Claudia.

"In Mexico I am four and a half. I don't know in the United States."

Cassidy and Lindsay both put their feet up alongside Claudia's.

"She looks the same size as me," said Lindsay. "Like a seven and a half."

"That's my size, too," said Cassidy. "I have an extra set of cleats and shin guards in my locker. We'll get you set up."

Lindsay was amazed. This was the friendliest she'd ever seen Cassidy before. What had come over her?

The first bell rang.

"The moment of truth!" said Cassidy. "I need to go to the bathroom to brush my hair and stuff. Wish me luck!"

Lindsay and Claudia both smiled.

"I'm sure you'll do fine," said Lindsay.

As Cassidy hurried inside, Lindsay and Claudia made their way more slowly into the building along with the throngs of other kids.

"Thank you, Lindsay," said Claudia, her eyes shining. "Even if I only play today, I am so happy to play again."

Lindsay smiled. "You're welcome," she said. "I'm sure you'll be awesome." She thought about how confusing and bad the past week had seemed. Imagine if all that confusion was happening and you were far from home, too. Lindsay hoped Claudia wasn't too homesick. "I'll come to one of your practices to watch," she said. "And one night you can come home for dinner with me." And before Claudia could protest she said, "And don't worry, I'm sure my mom will drive you home."

"Thank you!" said Claudia. "I'd like that." The girls smiled at each other and headed inside to hear all about Cassidy.

"MY NAME IS CASSIDY SINCLAIR."

The class had settled down after the morning announcements, and now Cassidy was up at the front of the room.

Lindsay looked at Nick. He was leaning forward in his seat, listening raptly to Cassidy, his strong arms looking fantastic in his polo shirt.

Does he have to look so perfectly amazing? Does she? Lindsay thought. Cassidy was wearing a slim-fitting T-shirt over a flippy pleated skirt with adorable patent flats. She wore multiple strands of silver necklaces, and she'd pulled back her blond hair and twisted it into an intricate bun in the back. It looked like she'd been to a salon to have her hair done.

Cassidy was doing the usual bit that everyone else had done, showing slides of herself as a baby. She flashed a slide of her parents, which looked like it had been taken a long time ago. Her mother wore a long evening gown, her father a tuxedo. They looked really young, almost like teenagers, except for their fancy clothes. Lindsay wondered if they were about to go to the opera or something. Cassidy looked a lot like her mother, who in the picture was blond and slim and beautiful.

"These are my parents, but I don't really get to see them very much. I, um, saw my dad two Christmases ago and I saw my mom, um, the last time, when I was four."

The class suddenly grew quiet. Not a chair shifted. Not a person coughed.

Cassidy took a deep breath and continued. "My parents divorced when I was a baby and my dad lives in France with his new family. I have a little half brother now. I've met him twice. My dad came to one of my games once and brought my half brother." She swallowed, looked down, and then looked up again with her bright smile back in place. "Anyway, now I live with my grandparents."

She flashed a picture of another couple. They were also very elegant, but they looked even older than Lindsay's own grandparents.

"That's my grandmother. She's my mom's mom,

but she also hasn't seen my mom in, like, years. She volunteers a lot for her, um, committees and she's always out at an event. And that's my grandfather. He likes to play golf. And he hates the cold weather and wishes he lived in Florida. He works a lot and gets home pretty late most nights."

The next several pictures were all of Cassidy on sports teams. Group shots of her on soccer teams, softball teams, basketball teams. But there were no pictures of Cassidy at birthday parties or on family vacations. There wasn't even one picture of Cassidy with another kid who wasn't a teammate.

Cassidy flashed a picture of another older woman standing in a fancy kitchen. The woman wore a uniform and an apron.

"This is Anna. She's been my best friend forever. She drives me back and forth to soccer and she comes to a lot of my games," said Cassidy. "She has a son in the marines and a daughter who lives in New Jersey and three grandchildren that she wishes she could see more often, but she also says I'm like her fourth grandchild."

There were just a few more slides, mostly of Cassidy

on more teams, and then she finished up. "So yeah," she said. "That's been my life so far. I hope someday to play professional soccer or maybe be in the Olympics!" She grinned as everyone clapped, and then the bell rang and it was time to go.

Lindsay felt all topsy-turvy. Cassidy wasn't the person she'd thought she was. As everyone filed out, she checked her schedule. Seventh grade had a much more complicated schedule than sixth grade, with her classes in a different order every day. Her first class of the morning that day was a study hall, in the cafeteria.

She walked in slowly and sat down at a table near the door, lost in thought about Cassidy's presentation. What a lonely life she'd led. Lindsay couldn't imagine how hard it must be to never get to see your parents. Where was Cassidy's mom, anyway? And she only met her half brother twice? And her dad lived a whole continent away with another family? *She must be lonely*, Lindsay thought. She pictured Cassidy eating dinner at home alone most nights. Lindsay could not concentrate on her social studies reading as she thought about it. It made her mind whirl to realize that someone as beautiful and popular as Cassidy Sinclair could have such big problems. She really didn't have the charmed life that Lindsay had always assumed she had.

Lindsay had misjudged her. She thought back on the conversations they'd had, where Lindsay had always jumped to the conclusion that Cassidy was being sarcastic. Maybe she wasn't! Maybe she genuinely was impressed with Lindsay's piano playing. Maybe she genuinely did like that "vintage" skirt she'd worn that day. And that comment about not caring what she looked like? Maybe Cassidy had meant it differently—like, she liked how Lindsay looked nice without seeming to have fussed over her appearance?

And then there was Nick. Nick, who whatever else you might say about him, was a very good judge of character. He wouldn't be going out with a stuck-up, mean girl. Clearly he had seen the nice side of Cassidy. Maybe Lindsay shouldn't have jumped to all those conclusions and been so quick to lose her temper with him. She sighed. That quick temper her mother reminded her about wasn't her best quality.

At lunch her old place at her friends' table, next to Rosie, was open again. She started toward it and then turned toward where Claudia was sitting, at the end of the other table as usual.

"Hey, Claudia," she said. "Want to come sit with me and my friends today?"

Claudia set down her sandwich and stood up quickly. "Thank you, Lindsay," she said. "That would be great. You are very kind."

Lindsay blushed. She didn't feel very kind. Lately she'd been a judgmental, fiery-tempered girl who spent way too much time assuming that the whole world was gossiping just about her. But she knew that wasn't who she was deep down. And that wasn't how she was going to act anymore.

"Hey guys, this is Claudia, in case you don't know her," said Lindsay. "Claudia, this is Rosie, Jenn, Sasha, Chloe, Ava, and Bella."

"Hi, Claudia!" they all said, and moved to make room for her to sit down.

Lindsay felt happier than she'd felt in days.

chapter 17

THAT AFTERNOON SHE AND DAVID COSTELLO MET at the band room to practice their duet. It sounded pretty good, she had to admit.

"Excellent," said David, after they'd played it through to the end twice. "There are a couple of tricky rhythms here, and here," he pointed at places in her music, "and you'll need to work on it in some places, but you've got a good ear for accompaniment and a nice touch."

"Thanks," said Lindsay. "You're pretty good too."

"Oh, and I told Mr. Thompson you'd be available for rehearsals for the musical, too," he said casually. "I think once he hears how good you are, he'll be pretty psyched to have you play for the performances."

Lindsay stared at him. "Thanks for letting me know!"

"You're welcome. Let's take it from the top one more—oh, hold that thought!" David said as something caught his eye. In one quick motion, he handed her his clarinet and headed toward the door. "Yoo-hoo, Tiffany! Wait up a second!" he yelled as he ran into the hallway.

Lindsay cringed. She remembered David saying that the name of the girl he was crushing on was Tiffany. Did he really just yell her name like that and *run* after her in the hallway? Lindsay crossed her fingers that whatever rejection David was about to endure would be quick and painless. He was a really nice kid, and she didn't want him to be totally crushed . . . especially in public.

But when David returned to the room a few moments later, he was flashing a big purple grin that spread from ear to ear.

"So what was that all about?" Lindsay asked, baffled by David's happy expression.

"I hadn't had a chance before now to ask Tiffany to the dance," David explained as he accepted his clarinet back from Lindsay.

"Um, what did she say?"

"Please, Lindsay. Did you not notice my smile? She

said yes, of course! How could she turn me down? I'm the best musician in the band. Tiffany is very smart. She knows a good thing when she sees it."

"She sure does," Lindsay replied, unable to stop herself from returning David's big goofy grin.

After they'd finished rehearsing and David had left, Lindsay stayed at the piano, lost in thought. She played a thoughtful piece, "Arabesque" by Schumann. As her fingers moved along the keyboard, she thought about Nick. How much she missed him. How she wished things could be back the way they used to be. More than they used to be. She could admit it now: She wanted to be more than just his friend. Unfortunately, so did every other seventh-grade girl at Central Falls Middle School.

She finished the piece and sat there quietly. A tear trickled down her cheek, and she didn't even bother to wipe it away.

"That was awesome," said a quiet voice behind her.

She wheeled around. It was Nick.

He was still in his soccer practice stuff, his goalkeeper shirt grass-stained and muddy, his black pants clinging to his long legs. Even in that outfit, he looked ridiculously good.

She quickly wiped away the tear from her cheek. Had he seen it?

"I had no idea you'd gotten so good at piano," he said admiringly. "I was pretty blown away when I heard you playing those kids' songs at the party on Friday, but that piece you were just playing is really . . . amazing. You sound like you could be a professional someday."

"Thanks," she said, and stood up, feeling self-conscious. Were her eyes red? Was her face puffy?

Nick stepped into the room, setting down the soccer ball he had crooked under one arm. "Hey, that was really nice of you to get Claudia to join the team. She's an awesome player, by the way. We scrimmaged with the girls' team at the end of practice. Her footwork is better than most of the guys on *my* team. The girls' coach is *psyched*. Claudia's totally going to become a dominant player."

Lindsay smiled. "I'm really glad. Cassidy was actually really sweet about inviting Claudia to join the team. I—you guys make a good couple." She almost choked on the words but managed to get them out without doing so.

Nick sighed, looked up at the ceiling, and then side

to side, as though he were trying to figure out how to say something. Finally he looked straight at her, his dark eyes looking like pools of chocolate. "Listen, Linz," he said. "You've got it all wrong about Cassidy. She's really a nice girl. She—"

"I know, I know," said Lindsay. "I really misjudged her. I thought she was really stuck-up because she always has new stuff and she doesn't talk to anyone except people on her team, and she didn't invite me to her party, but after I saw her presentation this morning, I realized she's had to deal with a lot, and I shouldn't have jumped to those conclusions."

"She's not stuck-up at all," said Nick. "She's really shy, actually. That may be why you think she doesn't talk to people not on her team. And yeah, her home life is pretty rotten. Her grandparents barely spend any time with her. She was raised by nannies and stuff."

"She just made a few comments to me that I thought were, like, sarcastic, but now that I think about it, maybe they weren't," said Lindsay.

"No, she really isn't a sarcastic person," said Nick. "And she's not my girlfriend, either."

"She was really—wait. What?"

The last thing Nick had said finally registered with Lindsay. Had he just said they weren't going out?

He was grinning that sideways grin and shaking his head. "No. We're not going out. We never were. I guess a few people thought we were, and I sort of let them think so because, well, it was kind of cool to have people think such a hot girl was interested in me. I guess I still think of myself as a little sixth grader that no one notices. Plus you were acting all aloof and stuck-up."

"*I* was acting stuck-up?" Lindsay's eyes widened.

"Well, yeah. You didn't even look my way that first day of homeroom. And at lunch I saved you a seat at my table and you walked right past, pretending not to know me."

Lindsay thought back, trying to remember. There *had* been an empty seat next to him. She'd just assumed he'd saved it for Cassidy—and that's where Cassidy had sat every day since then. How was she supposed to know he'd been saving it for her? "Well, why didn't you return my texts that I sent you?" she said accusingly.

"I told you, but you didn't seem to believe me. Ellie took my phone and I couldn't find it, and then we couldn't find where she'd put the charger. I didn't have my phone for almost a whole week."

"Okay, well, I didn't believe you because you'd lied to me about the other thing."

"*What* other thing?" he asked. "When did I *lie* to you?"

"Remember that day you said you had to get to practice? Well, I happen to know you didn't even have practice. My mom sent me in to find you, and I saw you talking with Cassidy in the hallway. You so didn't have practice."

Nick looked confused, as though he were trying to remember. Then he did. "We *didn't* have practice, not officially. But Cassidy had asked me if she could take some shots on me. Her Elite Team coach told her she needed to work on developing her left foot. So I told her I'd stay after that day so she could take some shots on me on the other field. Gee, Linz, you really jump to conclusions, you know?"

Lindsay started to say something about how cozy they looked, and then stopped. "You're right, I do. I'm trying, though." She swallowed. "I have no right to get mad at you for letting people think you and Cassidy were going out," she admitted. "I wanted you to think

I was going out with Troy because I thought it was cool that an eighth grader liked me. And I was mad at you and trying to annoy you. But it was a pretty rotten thing to do to Troy."

"Yeah, well, I guess we've both been pretty rotten," he said. "Anyway, not to worry. Troy asked Cassidy to the dance and she said yes, so all's well that ends well."

"That's awesome!" said Lindsay, genuinely pleased.

Nick scuffed the rug with his foot. "So Troy told me you told him you weren't planning on going to the dance. Is that, um, true?"

Lindsay caught her breath. What did he mean? Why was he asking? Then she calmed herself. This was just Nick, her friend, talking to her like old times. Relax. "Yeah, that's what I told him," she admitted. "Because I thought he was going to ask me and I didn't know what else to say."

"Well, so, uh, is there any way I can change your mind?"

"About Troy?"

"No, you dimwit. About the dance."

Lindsay blinked at him. "You mean, are you asking—"

"Duh, yeah. I'm asking you to the dance. Because I want to go with *you*. I want to go *out* with you."

Lindsay felt faint. She clutched the edge of a chair. She didn't trust herself to say anything.

Nick must have taken her silence for hesitation. "Okay, it's okay. You don't have to say yes. I know it's weird, since we've known each other since we were zero and all, and—"

"Of course I'll go with you!" she finally managed to blurt out. She practically jumped up and hugged him. She didn't know what to do with her hands. She grinned like a maniac at Nick, but she didn't care. Nick had asked her to the dance. Nick liked her!

Nick smiled back. "Awesome."

"Yeah, it's pretty awesome."

He cleared his throat. "So, you know how I have to give my presentation tomorrow? Well, I was so upset that you and I weren't getting along that I took out all the pictures of the two of us, and now all I have to show for my talk tomorrow is one ugly fat baby picture of myself."

She laughed.

"And so I was wondering, if you don't have too much

homework, if you could just come back to my house and help me put the pictures back in? My mom is coming to pick me up in about five minutes. I think she already told your mom you were coming with me." He blushed.

Lindsay laughed again. "Of course I will," she said. "But, gee, think of the gossip this is going to generate. We both have slides showing the two of us together and then we're going to the dance, too? Can you even imagine what people will be talking about?"

"I don't care if you don't care," said Nick.

And Lindsay realized she didn't care one bit.

Here's a sneak peek at the next book in the series:

Noelle's Christmas Crush

MOM IS TAKING ME BLACK FRIDAY SHOPPING. Want 2 go? texted Jessica.

Busy 2day, Noelle texted back.

Y?

U no y! *<<<<=

LOL! You are Christmas crazy.

I no. Have fun shopping!

Noelle smiled and put down the phone. Jessica had been her friend since they were little, so she should have remembered that the day after Thanksgiving was a special one for Noelle. It was the official start of the Christmas season, the most important time of the year! Well, at least to Noelle. And even if it wasn't the most important time of the year, it was the best time of the year.

I guess I am Christmas crazy, Noelle thought. But she had a good reason to be. Not only was she born on December 25, but her last name was Winters, and on top of all that, her parents had named her Noelle Holly. Noelle Holly Winters! She was destined to be Christmas crazy.

"Noelle, are you gonna just talk on your cell phone, or are you gonna help us?"

Noelle's teenage brother Andrew came in through the back door carrying a big cardboard box. She quickly slid her phone in her pocket.

"Okay! Okay! I'm helping!" Then she headed outside into the chilly late-autumn morning.

Mr. Winters was waiting in the driveway. "What do you say we get that tree? I want to get there before the good ones are gone. And we need some place to put all these ornaments!"

Noelle laughed. "We'll probably be the first ones anywhere to get our tree," she said, but she was excited.

Once the tree was up, it would feel like Christmas for real. And that would mean her birthday was getting close too.

The family bundled into the car and drove to the fire station in downtown Pine Valley. They always got their tree from the parking lot next door, because some of the profits went to the firehouse. Mrs. Winters popped a Christmas music CD into the dashboard.

"Might as well get into the spirit," she said.

It seemed to work, because Andrew and Noelle didn't argue at all on the drive (which only took ten minutes), and when they pulled up into the lot with all the trees stacked up by the metal fence, Noelle felt a big surge of Christmas spirit.

They climbed out of the car and searched the lot. Mrs. Winters stood back and watched; she knew her family well. Noelle and Andrew would each quickly find a tree that they were certain was "the best," but Mr. Winters would examine just about every single tree in the place until he found the perfect one.

And that's exactly what happened. Right away, Noelle found a tree with a round, fluffy shape, and Andrew went to the tallest tree in the lot.

"Dad! Dad! Over here!" they yelled.

But Mr. Winters methodically went through the lot, stopping to touch the needles of a tree, or standing back from it and looking at it with squinted eyes. Everyone waited impatiently until he finally called out, "I've got it!"

They circled around the tree he had propped up. It was tall, but not as tall as the tree Andrew had picked. It was round and fluffy, but not as wide as Noelle's tree. It was the very best of both. Everyone had to agree that it was perfect.

By the time the tree was tied to the roof, everyone was hungry, so they stopped at the drive-through and ordered a sack of burgers and four peppermint milkshakes, a special treat for tree-trimming day.

They spent the rest of the afternoon putting up decorations and hanging ornaments on the tree. Noelle carefully went through the box and picked out her favorites to hang, and Andrew did the same. It was kind of an unspoken agreement between them. Andrew got to hang the little wooden train and the pinecone ornament that he made in second grade, and Noelle got to put up her handprint and the little birds in nests that clipped onto the branches. The only one they ever argued about was the pickle.

This time, they reached into the ornament box for the pickle at the same time. They both stopped, and then Andrew shrugged.

"Go ahead," Andrew said.

Looks like someone has found the Christmas spirit after all! Noelle wanted to say, but she knew better. She just smiled and hung the pickle on the tree, right in the middle.

Mrs. Winters stood in the center of the room with her hands on her hips and inspected their work.

"Everything looks beautiful," she said.

Noelle looked around. A garland of green branches and berries was draped across the fireplace, and her dad's Santa collection adorned the mantel. The tree was lit with dozens of tiny white lights, and a big glowing star shined at the top.

"It's perfect," Noelle agreed.

Her mom smiled and shook her head. "Well, it *will* be perfect once we get all these storage boxes put away."

Mr. Winters sank into the armchair next to the tree. "Can we do it later? I was thinking of heating up the leftover turkey for some sandwiches for dinner."

“Yeah, we’ve been doing stuff all day,” Andrew added.

“Fine, then,” Mrs. Winters said. “Let’s take a break. I’ll call you when dinner’s ready.”

“I can work on my birthday party planning!” Noelle announced, and then she ran up to her room.

Last year she had received a laptop for her birthday, and it was the perfect gift—not just because it was pink. She had started right away planning the party for this year. She’d saved pictures of party decorations and cakes, and made lists of what she would need. She had also bookmarked a free site where she could make awesome e-mail invitations that she could send out to her friends.

She sat on her bed and turned on the laptop, going right to the invitation site. She had a tentative guest list working, but she hadn’t hit send yet. She stared at one name on the list: Noel Shepherd.

Just hit send, she told herself. *What’s the worst that could happen?*

But she chickened out, just as she had yesterday and the day before that.

Maybe tomorrow, she thought, and then she clicked over to the birthday recipe site.